A STORY OF WAR, SPIES...

AND A STOWAWAY

S●S LUSITANIA

In 1915, only three years after the
Titanic disaster, another liner, the *Lusitania*,
sank off the coast of Ireland near Kinsale, County Cork.
It was torpedoed by a German submarine.
Over a thousand people were drowned.

Kevin Kiely — poet, novelist, playwright, literary critic, American Fulbright Scholar, PhD in modernist poetry — was born in County Down, Northern Ireland. Books: *Quintesse* (St Martin's Press, New York); *Mere Mortals; Plainchant for a Sundering* (Lapwing)*; Breakfast with Sylvia*, winner of the Patrick Kavanagh fellowship 2006; *Francis Stuart: Artist and Outcast, The Welkinn Complex; Sweeney: Patron of Modernist and Postmodernist Poetry at the Woodberry Poetry Room Harvard 1942-1976*; 'A Map of Melancholy', long poem in *Windows* anthology, eds Heather Brett and Noel Monahan 2012. Plays on RTE: *Children of No Importance* and *Multiple Indiscretions*. His other novel for young readers is *A Horse Called El Dorado*, which won a Bisto Honour Award.

DEDICATION

To Laura and Ruadhán, my favourite storytellers

SOS
LUSITANIA

KEVIN KIELY

THE O'BRIEN PRESS
DUBLIN

First published 2013 by The O'Brien Press Ltd,
12 Terenure Road East, Rathgar, Dublin 6, Ireland.
Tel: +353 1 4923333; Fax: +353 1 4922777
E-mail: books@obrien.ie
Website: www.obrien.ie
ISBN: 978-1-84717-230-3

British Library Cataloguing-in-Publication Data
A catalogue record for this title is available from the British Library

1 2 3 4 5 6 7 8 9 10
13 14 15 16 17

Editing, typesetting, layout and design: The O'Brien Press Ltd
Printed and bound by CPI Group (UK) Ltd, Croydon, CR0 4YY
The paper used in this book is produced using pulp from managed forests

The O'Brien Press receives assistance from

CONTENTS

HOME IS
WHERE THE
HEART IS

CHAPTER 1

THE NIGHTMARE

Last night I had a terrible dream. My dreams and visions are a bit frightening because sometimes I can see into the future; nobody knows about this secret of mine, though often Mam is woken if I scream, and she calls out to me: 'It's just a bad dream, Finbar. Go back to sleep, son.' My younger brothers, Christopher and Sean, were sleeping soundly in the bunk beds that we call 'shelves'. 'Get up on your shelf!' we'd joke at night when they were going to bed.

In the dream, there was a shipwreck, explosions, flames. A huge ocean liner was breaking up and sinking into an icy sea. There were lifeboats and people screaming. I woke up, sweating.

It was the kind of nightmare that when you wake up

the events are still there. The water was rising up over my bed – but when my feet touched the dry, cold floorboards a feeling of calm returned. I stood at the window, staring at the gaslights outside on the sloping streets of Queenstown. I yawned for a while, then went back to my cosy bed. Everything became peaceful now, just rainwater from the roof sloshing down on to the streets.

I cannot really tell anyone my secret dreams, because sometimes these nightmares are like a message about what is going to happen days, weeks, or months later – but I never know if the events I see will *actually* happen. Like when our dog Rusty, a whippet, got lost … or stolen … or ran away. Days before it happened I had a dream that we were looking all over Queenstown for him. I forget the dreams that don't happen, but Rusty *is* gone. Surely the shipwreck is too fantastic to be true? Maybe I was just remembering the *Titanic* three years ago? I don't think it could ever happen again. It is too shocking!

But my father is away working on the *Lusitania*, one of the world's biggest liners.

Next day I dawdled coming out of the school yard when lessons were over. Seagulls swooped down looking for something to devour, birds with yellow beaks and webbed feet, pouncing on a squashed piece of bread that must have fallen out of someone's schoolbag. I stood staring at them, thinking about my wild dream, going over it in my head. The teachers stood near the turnstile gate. 'Chalky' Dempsey, nearly as tall as the spire on Queenstown cathedral. His grey hair was like a floor mop, his face the colour of a turnip, his ears like mushrooms, his suit forever dusty with chalk. The other teacher, Mrs Dempsey, his wife, was small and round as a bush, her black hair tied in a bun. She had tiny eyes, squinting out through spectacles. Sometimes I saw her at her sewing machine through their parlour window, and she was the same: squinting, stooping, sewing.

'Finbar!' My sister Colleen came running towards me, startling me out of my daydreams, her face staring wildly as she got so close we could easily bang heads. 'Dad is home. He's home!'

And she turned around and we both ran hell for leather up the steep hills of the town, jostling our way through the other kids and veering off the footpaths to avoid them.

'And he brought presents.' Colleen's voice was louder

than usual. 'It's like Christmas.'

We were both panting when we got to our house. Number 1 Park Terrace was redbrick, with black slates covered in green moss, and the gutter missing from half of the roof.

'Hey!' Colleen poked me in the stomach, her laughter like bagpipes starting up. She had gone all giddy. She pushed me aside and opened the front door.

'Dad is home!' she shouted and ran inside.

CHAPTER 2

TREASURES FROM CHINA

Mrs Kelly's hands and blue housecoat were flecked with flour. She was talking to Mam, who wore an apron also stained with flour. They baked pies for the shops and hotels downtown every week. 'Making a pretty penny,' Mrs Kelly always said. 'Well, it's a living – sort of.'

Mam hugged me, and I smelt the flour and dough off her. There were pies and tarts all over the place. The kitchen was warm with the smell of baking. It was the sweetest, happiest smell. Oh for some hot bread with butter – I couldn't wait. But where were the toys?

'Isn't it great your Daddy's home!' Mrs Kelly wore thick glasses that slid down her nose. She pushed them back up to her eyes and they looked like little windows with snow on them.

'They all missed him at Christmas,' Mam said to her. 'And I was lonesome without my Jack.' Mam pushed a strand of hair behind her ear. The flour got up there too. Mam put her floury hand on her waist, adding more white to the dark apron. 'Go into the parlour, Finbar. Wait till you see what your Dad brought. It's like a toyshop in there. He must have found buried treasure at sea to have paid for all those things. Christopher and Sean are in the park flying their kites. Your dad's gone down town. Ye'll all see him later.'

In the parlour our best table was covered in curious items. My mouth dropped open. Oh gosh, it *was* better than Christmas. We didn't have much of a time at the real Christmas, but now we could have it! Colleen was playing a little musical box that made sounds like a harp. I didn't know what to look at. My eyes roved over everything. Gosh, this was mighty.

'Mam says,' Colleen's eyes were wide, 'that Dad brought home all of China. All of flippin' China, can you believe it?' Colleen wound the spring on a clock and suddenly a bird popped out and hooted three times. 'Dad's the best in the world,' she shouted, her eyes shining with happiness.

'Here,' she threw me a postcard of a circus with elephants, and up on their backs were little huts with roofs! Chinese people were sitting under the roofs, wearing strange hats and smiling. Some of the smiling people looked up at birds flying overhead in the sky. On the postcard was a message from Dad. It was fantastic to read the postcard from him when he was already home with us, because it often made me sad getting the postcards when he's far away:

'Dear Kitty and all my cherubs,
We have been busy, busy. Leaving Hong Kong today and
missed the postbag going ashore. Bringing this to Ireland
– with myself!
Take care, from Daddy (Jack).

Here's a silly rhyme:
If a gumboil could boil oil,
How much oil could a gumboil boil
If a gumboil could boil oil?
I told you, it is silly! Big hugs for all. All for big hugs!

I held the card and grinned. Typical. I opened a box full of chocolate coins, wrapped in silver paper. I flicked off the wrappers and ate a coin. Eating 'money' made me laugh. A pretty penny! Chunky chocolate teeth were funny to unwrap and lovely to eat. Eating teeth with your own teeth! And what was over here? Lacquered black boxes that opened to the sound of insects. Chopsticks. Coins with four straight sides and a square hole in the middle. A toy boat with sails. Two boats with tiny oars. Balloons. Magic tricks.

Best of all, I found a spyglass with a label marked 'For my son, Finbar'. It was like a brass pipe, the bigger side with polished glass like the end of a bottle. I stretched it out, pulling both ends, and it was longer than a sword.

'Wow! Look, Colleen,' I shouted, but suddenly the front door was thrown open. The twins were back for more booty. Christopher was in a tussle with Sean as to who was going to get into the room first, so Mam separated them. Their clothes had flour stains now, but today no one was scolded. Mam rubbed the flour off them, pretending that she was beating them, and they were giggling.

'Hip, hip, hurray!' Christopher roared. 'I love all the goodies Dad brought.'

Then Mam gave out to us as we fought like cats and dogs about who owned which toys. Things got so noisy that Mrs Kelly rushed in – but moments later she rushed back out: 'My flippin' flaky pastry!' she shouted, and this seemed to stop us arguing and we all burst out laughing. We each stood at a corner of the table, our arms circled around our own bundle of toys. 'I don't want to hear another word of fighting about who owns what part of China,' Mam said crossly, but she soon began to smile again, and we began to cheer up. It wasn't a day for crossness. 'Ye're like a bunch of drunken sailors,' she said, tilting her head as she went back to her baking. The whole house was topsy turvy. But Dad was home. That was all that mattered.

Mam had an awful job trying to make us eat our carrot soup and brown bread and butter because we were so giddy and excited.

'You'll need to eat yours double-quick, Finbar,' she said. 'I'm sending you downtown to give your father a list of groceries to bring home.' She tore a piece of paper from the *Cork Examiner* and with a stub of a pencil wrote a list on it. I carefully placed the folded paper with flour stains in my pocket.

CHAPTER 3

THE LUSITANIA

Park Terrace is a long, level street that leads towards our school and beyond to the Corporation Park. I sauntered to the corner and turned down a sloping street, glimpsing the harbour with its two islands and the shining ocean. Out there on the water was the *Lusitania*, with its decks, black hulls and the four towering funnels like pillars. Could this be the ship in my dream? I couldn't be sure. How many ships are there in the world? Then the sky darkened and rain lashed the ground. I put my jacket over my head and started to run.

I checked to see that the shopping list was still in my pocket. I was really looking forward to seeing Dad after so many months. I hurried past the cathedral, lofty above the town and the harbour. The spire had a clock like a big eye looking down at me, a big, watery eye! I raced down the steep hills to the quayside. From down here the *Lusitania* was towering higher, like a giant mountain moored near the biggest island in the bay, Haulbowline. I'd seen the crane at Haulbowline drag a ship out of the water for repairs or for getting a fresh coat of paint after the ravages of the sea.

Suddenly the *Lusitania* gave out a whistle that stopped me in my tracks. It was a loud, low sound, like a sea monster howling in the night. How could anything awful happen to this great ocean liner? My Dad would not let anything destroy the *Lusitania*. Better find him and show him the shopping list.

The quays were busy. There were people everywhere – people who had just arrived, others preparing to leave in a day or two. The huge ship out there in the harbour made everyone stop and stare. I was excited as I slithered past families with mountains of luggage, even children carrying big bundles. These people stayed in the boarding houses along the seafront before travelling to America and England over the waves and far away. The rich people would stay in the hotels.

The Cunard Office in Westbourne Place was painted blue and red. It was really swanky inside, with flags hanging from the ceiling like bunting. Two lines of people stretched from the counters right to the back wall: passengers waiting to talk about their bookings and collecting their tickets to America; and workers from the *Lusitania* in the second line, chatting and pointing to documents and charts they held in their hands. All I needed to know was how to find Dad. I decided to queue with the people in uniform, and there were very few in front of me. At last a clerk called me to the counter with a smile and a questioning look on his face.

'Are you the Captain of the *Lusitania*?' he asked me, smirking at the others. They all laughed.

'No, but my father is Staff Captain,' I said proudly.

'Oh be japers! Who's your father when he's at home?' He stared at me with a quizzical look and took a pencil from his ear, rolling it in his fat, hairy fingers.

'Captain Jack Kennedy.'

'Jack Kennedy! Yerra boy, shake hands, son of Jack Kennedy,' a voice from behind me broke in, and I turned to see a bearded man whose peaked cap shielded his forehead. 'I am Bill Turner, Captain of the *Lusitania*.' We shook hands and he smiled warmly. 'Your father is in the Anchor bar. He has thirty-six hours' shore leave.'

I took my chance to ask him a question that was worrying me. 'The *Lusitania* ...?' I stuttered, staring at him, and he squinted down at me as if trying to read my thoughts. 'Is it the strongest ship that ever …?' My question seemed too dangerous to finish and fear gripped me.

'Do you not see her commanding the bay, boy? She's solid as the Rock of Gibraltar. That, sonny, is a great whale of a liner. I know her moods better than my missus's. Have no worries, son. And now, what's your name?

'F–F–Finbar Kennedy,' I said, stuttering again.

'Good day, Finbar,' he said with a bigger grin. 'Could your father walk the bridge of a better vessel? No, he's on the best – our most valuable Staff Captain, Jack Kennedy,' he declared. 'Proud to work with him, I am.' We shook hands again, and I ran out of the office, embarrassed, flustered and proud.

I walked along the street from the Cunard office in the rain and peered inside the first bar I passed, forgetting to check the name, and slowly went among the throng of people on high stools at the counter. Along the walls, gathered at round tables, were others with pint glasses full of frothy stout beside piles of empty glasses. The floor was covered in sawdust, with mud and cigarette butts scattered in it. Everyone was shouting in a chorus of voices, like a talking choir it seemed to me. The place had a sharp tang and smell of liquor that burnt my nose. It was a merry place, and the noise was terrific. The air was dense like a fog with the smoke of pipes, cigarettes and cigars.

At the counter, sailor fellas with slow voices and dramatic gestures talked to women dressed in brightly coloured clothes. In one corner a man played an accordion, tapping his feet as he shuffled the box in and out. It was lively stuff and made me feel like jumping around.

'What are you doing in here?' one of the barmen shouted, pushing a sleeve up his elbow and squinting down at me. 'What age are you?' he demanded.

'I'm looking for my father,' I shouted back at him. 'Is this the Anchor bar?' I had to say it many times while he held a hand up to his ear.

'Up the street, you gom! Dis is de Schooner,' he said finally. 'Can't you read? Go back to school, you *amadán*.' He jerked his thumb over his shoulder. 'Off with ya.'

Out on the street the air was cold and icy, and my eyes were watering after the smell of booze and smoke in that bar. It was still drizzling rain.

CHAPTER 4

DRUNKEN SAILORS

The Anchor bar was jammed to the door too. Halfway through the tide of drinkers I was nearly knocked down in the crush. It was going to be very hard to find Dad. Where was he? It took a long time to wade through to the back of the pub, but he was nowhere to be seen. On the slow return journey towards the front door I looked up into every face I passed. Next to the long counter was a little room, closed off with its own door. I pushed at it, but couldn't open it and no one came to my aid. Everyone was busy smoking, drinking and talking.

Suddenly I heard my father's voice – he was singing from the other side of the door, but then he was drowned out as others joined him in the song. Was it really Dad's voice? I was sure it was because I knew my father sang better than the birds.

Dress me up in me oilskin and jumper,
No more on the docks I'll be seen,
Just tell me old shipmates
I'm takin' a trip, mates,
And I'll see you some day
In Fiddler's Green.

I pushed hard on the door of the snug with both hands and it opened. There, in the middle of a throng, was Dad, a pint in his hand, and for a moment he looked like an actor on stage, holding everyone's attention. Then he saw me and his face lit up; he put down his glass and lurched towards me, nearly knocking over everyone between us.

'Shipmates!' he yelled, pulling me over to the blazing fire, 'this young man here is my eldest son, Finbar. Finbar, me boyo, come and sit here with your father. Oh it's good to see you, son.' He made room for me beside him. I took off my jacket and put it on the turf basket to dry off. He ordered lemonade, nuts, raisins and a bar of chocolate for me and put them on the mantel next to a line of empty glasses and bottles.

'What kind of a noise annoys an oyster?' Dad started with his old riddles, as usual. 'Come on, Finbar, you know what an oyster is?' he asked while the others listened to us.

'An oyster is like a dirty, fishy snail,' I answered, and they laughed, as did my dad.

'So, what kind of a noise annoys an oyster?' he still wanted to know, but gave the answer himself: 'Any kind of a noise annoys an oyster, but a noisy noise annoys an oyster most!' We all laughed and repeated it.

'Your father is leading us in a few songs, 'cos what else can sailors do with their land legs?' someone called to me.

This was my first time in such a place. I was used to meeting Dad outside some bar or other, or going in looking for him, but he had never brought me inside before. Today it seemed that he accepted me as part of his gang. I felt like a man as I looked at the tough faces all around me. Under the seats and chairs were yellow oilskins that were the brightest colour in this grey world of shipmen. One after another the sailors all handed me a coin, which made a good little stack. I thought about the shopping list, but could not bring myself to mention such a thing in their company.

'Finbar, we'll be going soon,' Dad said. 'Have the bit of a feast and enjoy yourself. Hey, Piper,' he called to a man sitting across from us, 'make it "Whiskey in the Jar". Our last song of the night.' But it took much more singing and farewells before we finally quit the Anchor. Outside the pub, Dad looked at the shopping list I handed him and nodded, flicking the paper as he called out each item: bacon, rashers, beans, head of cabbage, turnip, potatoes, tea, sugar, eggs, and sausages. But paying the outstanding bill at the shop would be the main thing, as usual. That would set him back.

'Dad, when are you off to sea again?' I wanted to know, not having fully understood Captain Turner's thirty-six hours' shore leave.

'We sail tomorrow night, son. The weather prospects are very good.' He glanced out at the *Lusitania* looming huge in the harbour.

'Dad! Can I take a day off school tomorrow?'

'Ah, you have to go to school, Finbar. Mr Dempsey would come rapping on our door and we'd be in trouble if we kept you out. Sure, I'll still be here tomorrow when you come home from school.' He stared at me and seemed to be begging me for courage.

'Dad,' I said, 'the spyglass is great. I really like it. Thanks.' I grabbed his arm for a moment, then he made a fist and I made one too.

'Ah sure, I'd bring ye back the whole world if I had a bag big enough,' he laughed, and his words sounded stuck together.

'Dad!' I said, 'I want to leave school and work on the

Lusitania with you. Can I? Please!'

'Well, you could, maybe. But you know you need more schooling first – a lot more, Finbar.' He smiled and put a hand on my shoulder. 'Wait a year or two, and if you have learned your books by the age of fourteen or fifteen, well, we might get you working as a cabin boy, or a bellboy. We'll see.' He looked at me, but I couldn't say anything.

'Very well, that's settled, so,' he announced. 'We'll all go to sea in a bath-shaped boat – the tinker, the tailor, the soldier, the sailor, the rich man, the poor man, the beggar man, the thief–'

'Dad, you sound a bit drunk. I hope you won't be singing for the people collecting their shopping.'

'There you go! You're a great lad protecting the old man from making a fool of himself.'

In Fitzgibbon's grocery, Mrs Fitz took the shopping list, and quickly began to clamber up and down to the shelves, using her footstool, to find the things we needed. I watched her cutting rashers and noisily slapping muddy potatoes onto the weighing scales. She shook rainwater out of the cabbage and carefully wrapped twelve eggs, each in a piece of newspaper, and filled a brown bag with them. 'Mind those eggs,' she said to me, raising a warning finger in the air and smiling at Dad who smiled back at her. Before we left, Dad went into her kitchen with her to pay out the money for our monthly grocery bill, while more people came into the shop. I saw Tommy Horgan, the messenger boy, come in to collect groceries. He gave me a smirk, but didn't talk as he was busy. In and out he went like a hare, carrying stuff until the double basket on the bike outside was filled. I envied him his job. He always had pennies. I stared out as he passed the window, pushing the bike, plodding along, with the 'Fitzgibbon Grocery' sign hanging from the bar between the wheels.

'So we still owe you?' I heard Dad whisper from the kitchen. 'Even though I've paid off the bill for January and February?'

'Look, Jack, it's fine. You can catch up,' said Mrs Fitz. 'Kitty and the kids have to eat. And she has to buy the eggs, flour and fruit for the bakery.' Her voice was kind.

'I know, I know,' Dad said, 'but I'm always in debt.'

'You're too good to your children, you spoil them – but, sure, why not? Ye'd better get home for the supper now. Say hello to Mrs Kennedy and Mrs Kelly. And I hear the ship sails tomorrow night for New York? You've got till the summer to clear your bill. Your credit is good, Jack.'

'Thanks, Mrs Fitz. I won't let you down. Thanks again.'

Mam was delighted to see us and we were all hugging each other for joy as if Dad had arrived home all over again! Mam and Dad put away the groceries in the dresser while I carefully unwrapped each egg and filled a bowl with them that rose like a tiny cove of round rocks that you would stack up at the seaside. My parents seemed to enter their own space in the kitchen as their voices blended together. Colleen, Sean, Christopher and I wandered into the parlour to look again at the toys and presents.

Then Dad put his head around the door. 'I'm going up to the turret,' he said. Colleen and I followed him upstairs, while Sean and Christopher stayed with the toys.

Up the narrow stairs we went, clumping noisily to the turret room, the attic that Dad had made for himself. He kept the stuff up here that he needed for his work. There were maps framed in glass on the walls, a writing desk where he kept his gun, a Smith & Wesson revolver, locked away when he was home from sea. His bookcase had glass doors and held a pair of binoculars, a twenty-four-hour ship's clock, a circular barometer, telescopes, parallel rulers, compasses, dividers, and logbooks, as well as nautical almanacs. Some of the shelves had the stories that he read, especially books by Joseph Conrad such as *Typhoon*. We sat quietly in the turret room, watching Dad go through all his things and sort out what to take with him tomorrow.

Then we got our homework done while our parents went out visiting since it was Dad's last night. It is difficult when your father works on a ship, I tell you. He's no sooner home than he has to go again. Mrs Kelly dropped in once to see if we were all right and later I heard my parents arrive with their friends, and the comforting sound of the voices downstairs lulled me into a deep, happy sleep. Oh why couldn't every night be like this?

The next day we all raced home as soon as school was over.

'Hey Colleen, wait!' I shouted as she ran ahead of me, but Christopher and Sean were winning the race home today. When I got to the front door my cheeks were really hot. I saw the others inside all clinging onto Dad who was dressed in his naval uniform. His leather case, with the letters JK, was ready on the kitchen table. I felt sad; the time for leaving had almost come again. Dad sat in his favourite armchair and gathered us around him. He began to tell stories and recite rhymes and riddles, and in no time he had the four of us in fits of laughter.

Two hours later, Dad poured himself a final cup of strong tea. Mam fetched a goose wing and brushed off his uniform, telling him that he 'might have creased it a bit with all the hugging and fooling around, but no bother.' There was an apple tart on the table. Dad talked non-stop while we all dived into the tart that was made specially for this supper.

At last Dad stood up. 'Now, shipmates, it's nearly time for me to set sail,' he said, pursing his lips and sighing. 'Sure, I hate to leave ye.'

Christopher and Sean were first to say goodbye as Dad tucked them into their bunks. Then he hugged me and Colleen before sending us off to bed too. He told me to be 'the man of the house' while he was away. Colleen was 'to help Mam as much as she could.'

Sitting on my bed, I took off my boots slowly and sadly, and was about to get into my nightshirt when Colleen passed the door. 'What's up, Col?' I whispered.

'I can't sleep,' she said, leaning against the door. 'I'm going to get a drink of water. Let's go and have a chat. Are the twins asleep?'

'They're out cold,' I said.

We passed the turret room with the five steps leading up to it and turned to tiptoe down the stairs when suddenly Colleen grabbed my hand. We sat on the stairs and heard Mam and Dad talking.

'Of course you had to tell me,' Mam said. 'I'm glad you have. How dangerous is it for you, Jack?' Her voice sounded anxious.

'You're not to worry yourself, Kitty, it's just with the war raging in France there are a lot of things we don't know.' Dad spoke slowly.

'Ah sure, I see the newspapers in the shops. They're full of pictures of soldiers and guns and planes. But it's so far away from us here in Queenstown we may as well be at the North Pole. We're safe as houses. But what about you, Jack? Do you think the *Lusitania* might be attacked?'

'There are rumours in the English and American newspapers,' said Dad. 'But our ship is the fastest afloat. Who could ever catch up with us? Besides, Kitty, I have to go. We're in debt.'

'I know, Jack, but you spend your money at the drop of a hat. Why did you bring so many presents home this time? I know you missed the Christmas, but the place is like a toyshop. You must think of saving ... but, sure, how can I scold you and you heading away now? Just come back to us in one piece, love. Mrs Kelly and I will bake our way out of some of the debt. And Mrs Fitz is good for credit.'

Dad sighed. 'Those toys were not too dear, Kitty. I got them all in the Chinese shop in Liverpool. I miss my darlings so much.'

'Just remember, Jack, ours is the happiest family on this street, even though you're away so much. Always remember that.'

Colleen dragged me by the wrist into her room. 'I'm worried for Dad at sea during the war,' she whispered. 'I don't understand the war. I hear Mam and Mrs Kelly talking about it but they hush up when I come along. And Mam got a bit cross today while Dad was down in the Cunard office. She said we are as poor as everyone else on Park Terrace except Dad sometimes has,' she stopped a moment, 'notions'.

'What?' I said. 'But Dad thinks he's going to be promoted sometime soon and he'll have bigger wages. Colleen, I really want to go to help him on the *Lusitania*,' I blurted out as we heard our parents going downstairs. 'I'm fed up of Mr Dempsey and I want to earn money.'

'Don't be silly, Finbar, you're only thirteen. Go to bed.' Her voice dropped and I could see she was sad and worried.

'But I have a plan,' I muttered.

'Finbar,' she said and yawned, 'we have school tomorrow and Dad has to go back to his ship. Good night!' She pushed me out of the door.

But I couldn't sleep. Later I crept back like a tomcat to sit in the darkness a safe distance from the light in the kitchen. How could I sleep tonight? If I had a nightmare after Dad left I would feel more miserable than ever. I leant against the stair railings and looked down at the table where I could see a large white envelope with the words *Cunard Line* printed above a drawing of the ship. I knew these envelopes well. They had the names of the Cunard ships printed in a row with a dash between each one: *Lusitania — Ordune — Tuscania — Transylvania*. I saw Dad's hand pick up the envelope.

I was afraid to go down, and when I finally did, Mam was there alone, with her arms folded, staring at the floor.

'Your father is gone,' she said with a catch in her voice. 'And you're a great boy, Finbar. A great comfort to me.'

'I love you, Mam.' The words would hardly come out of my mouth, and she held me tight for a long while.

'Oh look at the time, Finbar,' she said finally. 'It's after ten and you have school in the morning!'

'Goodnight, Mam,' I said, and rushed up to bed.

I had a plan and I was going to put it into action.

ALL ALONE
ON THE
HIGH SEAS

CHAPTER 5

RUNNING AWAY FROM HOME

Upstairs in the bedroom my mind was in a riot. Dad's visit had unsettled me like never before, and only now did I realise how difficult Mam and Dad's lives were. Dad said I must be the man of the house. So I will be a man, I thought, and why not tonight? This was my plan: I had decided to run away from home and get a job. As I was too young to work in the pubs and hotels in Queenstown, I would try to get work on the *Lusitania*.

First, I had to wait for Mam to settle down for the night. She could hardly stay up much longer after such a busy day. I heard her footsteps up the stairs at last, then she moved about in her room for a while before there was silence. I needed to leave the house quickly if my plan was going to work. I was careful not to wake my brothers and sat quietly on my bed waiting until everything in the house was totally still.

Then, near the window in my room, with the aid of the gaslight outside in the street, I began to write: '*Dear Mam, don't kill me but…*' I wrote clearly where I was going and what I was going to do, and I put the note under my pillow on top of my schoolbooks with the money I had got from the men in the Anchor. When I looked into the darkness at my brothers, my plan filled me with resolve.

What should I bring, I wondered? A warm jumper, socks, my penknife – what about my favourite things: the little boat Dad made me for my tenth birthday and the conker that was unbeaten among my schoolmates? I put the lot into my schoolbag and tiptoed down past the steps to the turret room, past Colleen's room, and lastly my parents' room at the top of the stairs. Crazily, I felt Mam might hear my loud breathing. Downstairs I pulled on my cap and grabbed my gabardine coat. I let myself out into the street, shutting the door with a gentle snap of the latch.

The town below in the distance was bustling as if there was a carnival or a fair in progress. This was always the way when a liner was either about to dock or depart from Queenstown. The rain was like a thin curtain as I ran – past St Colman's Cathedral that was blacked out except for the gas lamps like ghosts along the railings, down Chapel Street that curved around the cathedral, along Westbourne Place that faced the harbour, where I could see shuffling crowds in a long queue outside the main shipping building near the railway station.

The runners and touts were everywhere, busy carrying luggage in both hands. I knew all the touts and on a night like this I had often joined them and earned a few coins carrying luggage and helping passengers who were heading for the liner. You had to be 'in the know' to get this work and I hadn't got much recently. Tonight I would try harder. I had to get some luggage to take out to the *Lusitania*, otherwise my plan was ruined.

Out in the bay, beyond the island, I caught a glimpse of the *Lusitania* and I stared at it anxiously. It looked huge, full of strength and power and it made me feel like a little elf. The liner looked like a village in the distance, with its lights and the smoke coming from the huge chimneystacks. Did my future lie out there?

Out of breath, I trotted along Westbourne Place, bumping into people everywhere. The bars were full and the

Commodore Hotel had a jazz band playing music inside the window. In the pubs there was fiddle and accordion music, loud talking, and drunken singing. In the cafés, people were eating and drinking, while sailors played cards silently, with poker faces. The street was blocked by a mob around a fistfight between two young men near the Yacht Club. I wanted to watch, but I moved past them. I was on a mission.

The railway station rumbled into life with the arrival of a train. Sparks came from the chimney of the engine. In the Emigrant Office every door was open. The place was full of people, their shadowy faces and their ghostly frames made real only by their talking. Inside, a huge throng was waiting in line – men, women and children. In the dimly lit hall, everyone had luggage – but not schoolbags I noticed. So I decided to conceal my schoolbag; I pulled my arms through the straps, then squeezed and dragged, trying to get my gabardine coat on over it. When I finally got my arms through the sleeves they were halfway up my elbows. I walked a bit like a hunchback, but there was no other way.

'Hey Finbar, you fool, you look funny with the coat! Is there a monkey on your back?' Tommy Horgan bumped into me, flashing coins as he opened one hand. 'Did your Ma let you out for some touting? I saw your Da going out on the first tender. I worked all afternoon for Fitz's. There are a few rich yanks over there,' he winked. 'Should be good for tips.'

It was good of him, but I wondered was it too late already. I was beginning to panic about my plan to run away. Was it a stupid idea?

'The last of the passengers are over there, so now's your only chance.' Tommy pointed towards the ticket desk, a long counter where there was a small queue of toffs wearing coats with fur-trimmed collars, and fine brogues and hats.

'Thanks, Tommy. I better go off and see can I earn a coin, so,' I said, and grinned at him to hide my worries. Inside, I was not sure if I could follow through with the plan at all. I decided to forget the whole thing and go home. The plan was crazy. Leaving home as a stowaway on board the *Lusitania*! Was I cracked in the brain, or what?

A voice broke into my thoughts. 'You, boy! I want you to work for me. I will give you five dollars.' It was an elderly woman with white hair. I jumped. Her accent was foreign: *I vant you to vurk far mee. I vill giff you fife dollarz*, was what she really said. Her clothes were black and she stood beside a four-stack of luggage in decreasing sizes.

I stuttered. 'Five doll…dollars? Yes. Okay.' It was a good tout. I touched my cap and looked into her powdered face.

'Are you going on the night sailing?'

'Of course! How else can I get to New York?' I felt a bit silly for asking. 'There is my luggage, boy!' She pointed as if I were a simpleton.

'Righty-o,' I said. I grabbed the smallest cases and put them under my arms, then bent to lift the bigger ones. Her luggage was really heavy. No wonder she was offering five dollars!

A man in a peaked cap spoke through a loudhailer. 'All the passengers must board the last tender. Last tender now boarding!' he bellowed, loud as a foghorn. The line of passengers began to move slowly forward and with them the touts, me included. My mind was totally on the task of lifting the cases. The woman walked beside me and seemed anxious about her luggage; she kept looking at it as if counting the number of suitcases all of the time.

'This boy is working for me,' she croaked in her foreign accent (*ziss boy iss vurkink far mee*) to the ticket man as we shuffled towards the quayside. A sharp blast of cold air rose from the dark sea, refreshing and salty.

'Very well, Madam.' The man in uniform had his arms stretched out, keeping the line moving.

The tender took passengers and their luggage to and from the *Lusitania* with other supplies. It was much bigger than a rowing boat, with lots of seats on deck and a small engine house in the stern. The old woman balanced herself with an arm over my shoulder as we went unsteadily along the gangplank. It was difficult passing the luggage down into the bobbing boat, but a man helped me and placed it in the boat. The tender was tied up and straining against its moorings, and I was suddenly conscious of the great power of the sea. The woman and I sat together with the luggage between us. She had one arm stretched across two suitcases and she told me to hold the others. She is fussy, I thought!

At last a sailor loosened the tow-ropes from the steel bollards, and the engine started to throb and hum as it veered towards the great dark mass of choppy sea. The lights of Queenstown grew dim and far away, and the cold night air made me shiver. My plan had worked so far and despite the ache in my back from the schoolbag under my coat and from lifting the luggage, at last I began to feel a sense of great excitement. I was on my way!

'What is your name?' the lady asked.

'Finbar.' Speaking seemed to make her less anxious, so I asked politely, 'And what is your name, Ma'am?'

'Please hold on to the luggage. Please!' she said bluntly, ignoring my question.

CHAPTER 6

A PLACE TO HIDE

The persistent smell of seawater gradually changed and became mixed with the heavy fumes of burning coal as the tender approached the *Lusitania* that looked ghostly in the night except for the sections lit up on deck. Soon we were alongside, tying up to a floating jetty and above us was the great black wall of the liner with loud, humming engines droning and wailing, making ready for the voyage. The huge hull blotted out the stars in the sky that twinkled as if they were hanging from the mesh of deck railings. I heard voices and saw faces peering down.

The jetty had a gangplank that sloped upwards and this wide stairs was the means of boarding the liner. Passengers moved up the gangplank, holding on to ropes while the touts that carried the luggage moved more slowly under their load. The foreign lady suddenly seemed more relaxed as our turn came. She went ahead and I plodded after her with the luggage. It was bad enough on the flat jetty, but each step upwards was a bit scary as I was worried I might fall backwards, luggage and all. I took each step slowly and managed to keep my balance. The lady was on deck first, watching me closely, and as soon as I had made it aboard she called me to stop, almost as she would a dog: 'Halt!'

The steward, who held a lantern, examined her ticket; it was like a little jotter of printed yellow pages, and bore the words FIRST CLASS. 'Baroness von Leiditz, welcome aboard. Your first class cabin awaits you,' he said with a deep bow, and the pages of her ticket flapped in the breeze. He took a key from a wooden box and handed it to her. 'Stateroom 13. There are signs along the way. It is not very far. Take the promenade deck until you reach the lounge and music room, then go down a half-flight of stairs.' He gave me a sharp look and jerked his head in the direction of her cabin. 'Do you know the way, boy?' he asked. I nodded, suddenly realising that running away from home would mean telling a few lies.

The Baroness waited for me to raise the load of luggage, then we headed for the promenade deck. The lounge was thronged with people, and in the music room there was a bandstand where musical instruments lay on chairs and band members stood around smoking.

Sure enough, after scuttling down the small staircase we reached a wide door marked 'Stateroom 13'. The Baroness clicked the lock and opened the door, and I nearly fell in with my heavy load. She turned up the gaslights in front of a mirror and the cabin glowed in a warm light. It was like our livingroom in Park Terrace, except the table, chairs and sofa were more posh. There were shelves with magazines and books and lots of cupboards. A bottle of liquor and two glasses stood on a side table. Ahead were two doors and between them was a mirror the same size as the doors. On one door was the word 'Single', on the other, 'Double'.

'I will pay you the five dollars after you do one more task,' the Baroness announced. She went into each room, put on the lights, rummaged around and came out. I noticed she had other keys which she must have found inside. 'I want you to divide the luggage between the two rooms.' She looked at each suitcase for a few moments. 'Yes. Take these into the single room.' She tapped two of the suitcases with her fingernail. I carried the suitcases into the room on the left, resting them against the single bed. There was a chair, a cupboard, and framed photographs of liners on the wall. I heard her speak again and hurried out. 'Now, these suitcases in there,' she pointed to the double room. 'That will be my room and this is all I need until I reach New York,' she explained slowly, becoming friendly for a moment.

The double room had a wide bed with a lamp on each side, lots of pillows above the neatly folded-back sheets and blankets, as well as a colourful covering that looked like a flag touching the floor on three sides. There was a mirror in front of a low table. Two chairs. Two cupboards and a big door marked 'bathroom', beyond which I glimpsed a bath, a basin and a toilet. The window even had curtains. It was like a room in a palace, fit for a king and queen.

Outside, the Baroness took out a small purse that had stitching on it of a black eagle with outstretched wings. 'Here,' she said, and handed me a crisp, green banknote.

'Thank you, Ma'am,' I said, unable to remember her long name and stuffed the money in my pocket.

'Now, boy,' she said, 'I need to send a message urgently. I will give you another dollar if you help me find a cabin steward.' She yawned and sat at the table. Opening a drawer she took out a pen, a folio with notepaper and envelopes that had the word *Lusitania* printed on them, along with a picture of the liner with its four funnels. 'One final task and then off with you, boy.'

'Yes, Ma'am.' I happily crinkled the five dollar bill in my pocket and watched as she wrote. I stared at the large handwriting and the number that she formed, using the delicate fountain pen: LVSTANA=397. She folded the paper with a swift glance at me, but I just stood there and looked dumb. She wrote a name on the envelope and pushed the notepaper into it.

We went out of her cabin, leaving the door unlocked. Then a very unfortunate thing happened. As we moved about in the throng of people looking for a steward, I suddenly spotted my father at the end of the corridor. He was examining some documents and signing them, while two stewards waited for them.

I went into shock. What would I do? I needed a place to hide – and quick!

I let the Baroness go ahead of me, then I slipped back quickly towards her cabin. It was the only thing I could think of. I darted back in through the cabin door. I could not let Dad see me. I would plan my next move in the cabin.

CHAPTER 7

THE GERMAN CODEBOOK

No sooner was I inside the cabin than there was a loud knocking on the door. I ran into the small bedroom and shut the door. It was dark, but I didn't dare switch on the light – anyway, light from the main room streamed through the slats in the door. I gazed out – it was like looking through my opened fingers.

Then, suddenly, I heard a deafening noise like thunder as the liner began to heave and sway. The pit of my stomach reeled as I realised that we had set sail for America! There was no going back now. I was a stowaway and I was on my way to New York. I sat on the bed and put my face in my hands. What would I do now? Where would I stay for the voyage without running into Dad? How long did it take to get to New York?

My mind raced in panic with questions I could not answer.

I was jerked out of my panic by laughing voices as people entered the cabin. I crouched close by the bed thinking it must be my dad and the Baroness. So the game was up and I would have to face punishment. I deserved it for running away from home.

'Oh that is so funny, Mr Crowley,' the Baroness was saying. 'You were knocking on my cabin door and I was knocking on your cabin door.' She slammed the door to the corridor with a loud bang.'I have lost that boy who was supposed to be helping me. No matter! I do not need him now.'

'And have you the German codebook?' I heard the man's booming voice on the other side of the door. I tried not to move a muscle.

'Well,' she seemed hesitant, 'I will give it to you in New York.'

'But in Berlin, Baroness, you told me you would get it. I need it now. I must crack that code.' His words came out slowly and he sounded very annoyed.

'The codebook – the *Signal Buch der Kaiserlichen Marinerkehrsbuch*, as we call it – is most valuable. I must be sure of proper arrangements. We will sort it out in New York.'

'Really, Baroness, it will take a long time to understand the code. I want to work on it now on the journey. I have told you that my superiors will pay two million pounds in gold for it.'

As I listened my mouth grew dry. Cold sweat came out on my forehead and my hands shook. I knew I was hearing information that was dangerous. I didn't really know what a codebook was, but two million in gold meant that this codebook was very valuable indeed.

'Two million! But in Berlin you told me the British Secret Service would pay millions for the codebook. Two million is nothing. I am giving you the secret codebook of the German Imperial Navy. This is a most important document. I am committing treason by giving this to you. For two million? I do not think so, Mr Crowley.' Her voice was sharp and rasping like a machine that needed oil.

'You agreed to two million, Baroness von Leiditz.' His voice boomed too.

'Mr Crowley, I am giving you the German Navy's secret codebook to allow the British Navy to win the war – and you are offering me only two million! Is that plain enough for you to understand? I will wait till New York when you can get me more money.'

'We have our other business to attend to, of course. Let me go to my cabin, Baroness, and I will bring along a suitcase with samples of the merchandise you wanted to purchase.' He spoke in a quieter voice.

'Very well,' she said, almost in a whisper, and let him out the door.

What was I hearing? I had been thrown into a dangerous world of codebooks and war. I heard the Baroness moving into the bedroom next door. Then she came back out and approached the room I was hiding in. I curled up on the floor and closed my eyes tight. Suddenly I heard the key snap shut in the door. I was locked in!

A short time later there was a loud knock on the cabin door again. I decided to peep through the slats this time and saw the outline of a man dressed like a circus ringmaster, with a top hat, a black tailcoat, a shirt with a wing collar and a colourful bow-tie. He was carrying a suitcase that must have been really heavy because he gasped as he put it down. Then I noticed a cane in his other hand, with an egg-shaped knob and a steel spike at the end.

'Well, open it!' ordered Baroness von Leiditz.

He took out two guns and put them on the floor. I could see them clearly. They were made of black iron, with wooden handles and triggers like teeth.

'A Vicker's Light and a Bergmann,' he announced. 'You

can trust me, Baroness von Leiditz. Here are the weapons you wanted to see.' Crowley grinned with an evil face and took off his top hat to mop his brow with a handkerchief. I noticed that his head was bald, a great dome of pink flesh above his ears.

'I don't trust spies,' the Baroness said firmly.

'Are *you* not a German spy?' Crowley said. 'How do I know that the codebook is real? We *have* to trust each other, Baroness, to get our business done in New York. You sell me the codebook and I get you the gold. I introduce you to the arms dealer and you set up that deal you wanted for the von Leiditz dynasty to supply the German Army with extra weapons like these. Simple. Then your family is back in with the Kaiser, and all is well.' He sat down, and the bulk of his weight filled the narrow, upright chair.

'The von Leiditz dynasty is bankrupt,' she confided sadly. 'We did not get the contracts from German High Command to make battleships. My brothers are in the reserve army riding horses and training soldiers for the battlefields. It is an insult to our great family. My father is a great man. He sits all day lamenting our loss. Our name is superior to the von Tirpitz family, you know, or to any other military family. And my dear sister had to marry below her dignity and below our family dignity.'

'Really, Baroness, this is getting very far away from the business in hand.' Crowley sat upright.

'You want to know about the codebook, Mr Crowley?'The Baroness sounded as if she were going to weep. 'My sister married the despicable Kapitän Walther Schwieger, the scruffy captain of a submarine. What a disgrace to our family!'

Crowley shifted impatiently, but realised that he needed this information.

'Kapitän Schwieger was on a week's leave in our castle,' she continued. 'What a low person he is. One night he spoke too much over the wine at dinner – he spoke of the codebook. While he and Monika, my sister, were out horse riding I found the codebook in his luggage. I stole it and then I burned their little chalet to the ground – Father had given the chalet that is near the lake on our estate to Monika as a wedding present for her and Schwieger. Everything was destroyed, but once he knew that the codebook was burnt I saw the relief on his face. He would be able to get a copy at the naval base in Wilhelmshaven.'

'Baroness von Leiditz, you are a very determined woman,' said Crowley, knotting his fingers and cracking his knuckles. 'I will be staying at the Algonquin Hotel in New York. Room 666. On examination of the codebook, my New York contact,

Roger Maguffin, will pay you. We will have to agree on the price. But let us leave that until we meet again.'

Suddenly I sneezed loudly. They stopped talking immediately. And if that wasn't bad enough, I fell against the door because my legs had got pins and needles from being in the same position for so long. In a flash, Baroness von Leiditz snapped the key on the door and I fell into the room at their feet.

CHAPTER 8

SERIOUS DANGER

'Boy!' shouted the Baroness.

I scrambled to my feet. The guns lay between us in the middle of the floor, and the room seemed very restricted and horribly uncomfortable all of a sudden.

'You have a son?' Crowley exclaimed, looking at me and her in surprise. 'Can we trust him? How much does he know?' He sounded furious.

'He is only the luggage boy,' the Baroness said, pursing her lips. 'He should be ashore. He should not be on the liner. He is trouble.'

'Oh, we have a small problem then!' Crowley screwed a fist around the top of his cane as if he would break the white egglike knob.

'I think we have a big problem,' the Baroness said anxiously. 'It is dangerous for me travelling to New York because of the business I am doing.' Her voice seemed to echo off the cabin walls.

I felt the room heaving and moving more than it actually was. Things had gone totally crazy. I will die here, I thought.

'He has heard everything. Look at his face. In my work this is called an intelligence leak, Baroness.' Crowley stared at me as if I had escaped from the zoo. 'We'd better sort it out. I can dispose of him out the porthole into the sea. It is night-time, the liner is moving fast. No one will hear or see anything except us.' He fingered the top of the cane, ground his teeth and I was suddenly more scared than I had ever been in my life.

'I shall pour myself a glass of wine. Do what you have to do. And be quick.' The Baroness did not look at me.

Suddenly my fear turned into action. Crowley looked like a giant, but I rushed forward, kicking him on the shin, and grabbed the cane. But he clung onto it. I managed to pushed him backwards – then the cane jerked out of my grip with a single gunshot that shattered the mirror between the two bedroom doors. In the struggle, Crowley lost his footing, fell on the Baroness, and knocked over the table as well as the bottle and the glasses. I did not wait. I rushed past them out the cabin door, thinking how sinister it was that the cane was also a gun.

'Stop that boy!' I heard Crowley roaring from behind me. But he was a heavy man and I was far faster than he was. I reached the end of the corridor and bumped into a man with a moustache, who was smoking a cigar, while the woman who held his arm moved against the wall to let me pass. They ignored Crowley's shout. I saw a sign saying 'stairs' below the image of a hand, and bounded down the steps, nearly landing in a heap at the bottom. What had I seen and heard from Crowley and the Baroness? Dangerous stuff all right. I had to get into hiding – and quick. Crowley would be looking for me everywhere. I raced down to the next deck in leaps and bounds, and struggled out of my coat because sweat was pouring off me. It was a relief to pull the schoolbag off my back, but awkward carrying it and the coat. A woman asked me something about 'E Deck', but I ignored her and kept moving. Crowley might find me; the Baroness might find me; Dad might find me. Oh God! Leaving home gets you into serious danger, I thought.

Down I went, another four flights. I seemed to have lost Crowley. I turned on to a corridor where a heavy steel door bore the word 'cargo'. I stopped, and stood there gasping, holding my schoolbag and coat. Then, suddenly, the door opened. Someone came out, left the door ajar, and walked in the other direction. I rushed through. It seemed like a good idea – anyway, it was my only hope. There might be other doors out of it, I thought.

It was a storage room. I went past shelves of luggage, boxes, parcels and crates of all sizes that were stacked on the floor. The cargo seemed to go on and on. All around the walls were dimmer lamps, their wicks inside glass globes. There was a sloping desk with a lamp at each side, and inkbottles, pens and open ledgers. Then I heard footsteps coming and I ran into a dark, murky corner between shelves. A crewman came in, whistling, sat at the desk and started to count. 'Eighty-four plus nineteen plus twenty-seven,' he went silent for a moment as his belly rumbled and he burped, 'equals one hundred and thirty, plus seventy nine.' He counted again, 'Two hundred and nine.' I heard the ledgers slam shut, then his footsteps as he went to the door which slammed shut too with an echoing thud. A key was poked into the lock outside and turned with a very loud click. Except for the spluttering gaslights, the place became a vast, gloomy cargo area.

Crowley will hardly find me here, I thought, but I was

locked in again. I put my hands up to my face, closed my eyes and stared at the millions of tiny dots of panic that I saw in the inner darkness.

CHAPTER 9

IN A DUNGEON

The cargo dungeon, as I began to call it, was bewildering. I was desperate to get out, but the door was made of thick steel and locked. The handle was a bar of steel too. The liner was rising, falling and pitching with a lurch that made it heave before rolling back, and this rhythm was constant. It was difficult to keep my balance when I walked around. I lay down behind shelves of luggage – parcels, suitcases, bundles and packages – hoping someone, but not Crowley, would come and free me. I thought of Dad and Mam, Colleen and my brothers. But none of them could help me now, except Dad if he came to check the cargo. I was thinking that Mam would be upset in Queenstown and that she'd be worried sick about me.

It was a crazy, stupid, mad thing to do, to run away from home. What kind of a boy runs away from a happy home? I felt sleepy from all of the woe and didn't care anymore about anything. I started to cry, sobbing aloud, my chest heaving like the liner. Then I grew tired of the crying and decided to lie down, using my schoolbag as a pillow, with my coat as a blanket, even though my shoes were sticking out the bottom.

I woke up after some time – maybe a few hours – and heard two distinct noises: one was the loud booming of the liner, rolling, creaking and shuddering with all its power and might; the other was a scratching noise. The shuddering made me uneasy as if the liner was about to stall or lose power. How long had we been at sea? I did not know. Had I slept a whole day without noticing? I did not know. The place was stuffy. There was a dim light coming from a porthole behind some shelves. I made my way in the gloom to the desk; walking across the floor was like climbing a hill that kept moving about. I opened the ledger, but the pages were dark and unreadable without more light. I tried to light the lamps, but I couldn't.

The scratching noise came again. It made me stop and listen. I got closer to where it came from and stamped my foot. A grey rat, with its ropey tail and sleek body, scurried away. I immediately lost my nerve for sleeping on the floor. I moved towards the door, sat on the chair, lifted the heavy ledger from the desk and held it up, waiting to drop it on the rat. But after a long time the rat still hadn't come back, so I put the ledger down.

I went over and touched the wall and felt the studs of the rivets that held the liner together. Dad had told us about rivets. There was a regular pattern of rivets spreading out in every direction. My face and forehead felt cool against the wall and the drops of moisture were abundant. I wet my hands in the drops and bathed my face. I began to lick the wall to satisfy my thirst. The dryness of my tongue eased after much licking, and I was able to swallow without my throat sticking. I felt a bit better, and went back to the chair, steadying myself a few times since the liner was really thrusting forcefully ahead. I felt all right until the horrible rat made another appearance.

The creature slithered and circled the floor, making for the desk, so I had to challenge him. I lifted the ledger and he began to squeal. I flung the ledger with a steady aim – and missed. I grabbed the chair to defend myself. It was him or me. This was going to be our war. Again, he scurried away at my show of strength and didn't reappear.

The moisture on the walls kept away my thirst. I lifted the ledger and the schoolbag on to the desk and crawled up on top, dragging my coat over me. It made for a very uncomfortable sort of bed, but a deep sleep finally came over me. When I woke, my throat was sore. I was trembling with the cold and my chest ached. As I lumbered towards the wall, I felt weak and the motion of the liner toppled me – I hit the floor hard. It really hurt. Still, when I dragged myself up on to my hands and knees, the droplets of water on the lower rivets were in good supply. I licked and sucked as much as I wanted, but began to break into a wrenching cough.

I flopped on the floor in a weakness. If the rat came again, I could do nothing. Tears welled up in my eyes. My arms were heavy. My breathing was slow and painful. This was real big trouble. I was going to die and the rat would eat pieces of me every day. No one would know what had happened to me, ever. What could I do? In school, Mr Dempsey would write on the board for everyone in the class to learn off: 'Finbar Kennedy ran away from home. Pray for his safe return.' Queenstown seemed to have disappeared like a sweet dream. And America was as far off as Heaven. I missed my family so much it hurt. Crowley would be looking for me too. If he found me I was dead anyway.

My fear of the rat kept me between sleeping and waking. I was not going to let a measly rat kill me when I had escaped being shot by Crowley. I scolded myself for having ever run away from home. I suddenly began to croak and then tried to scream: 'I am Finbar Kennedy. Help me!' The only one that heard me was the rat, who moved every time I screamed. I raised my head and screamed more, but my screaming simply made the rat move around. Each time I raised my head and screamed, he moved. This was the end. I was going to die. I started to howl like a baby for his mama.

CHAPTER 10

FINBAR KENNEDY: MISSING PERSON

═══════════════════════════════

Christopher, Colleen and Sean, along with Mam, sat in the Royal Irish Constabulary Barracks in Queenstown answering questions for Sergeant Kilroy who wore his black uniform, with shiny buttons and a belt around the waist, standing in front of a map of County Cork. His peaked cap was on the desk, and beyond, through the window, lay a splendid view of Queenstown harbour on a bright, blustery April afternoon.

'Well, well, well,' said Sergeant Kilroy, and he stroked his chin as Mam sobbed, 'this is very distressing. Three days and no sign of your Finbar? I have put the Missing Person posters up around the docks. The police have them around Cork too, and we wait in hope. We have sent officers to the houses where Finbar's friends live in the town, and Mr and Mrs Dempsey at the school have been most helpful going from door to door with inquiries. Canon Gill will be saying prayers on Sunday in the cathedral for Finbar's safe return. Have you thought of anywhere else he might have gone besides the list of places you already gave us, Mrs Kennedy?'

'No,' she replied, sighing. 'You have heard from my sister, Mary, in Youghal. Finbar is not with them. Will you be searching Cork city?' she pleaded, folding and unfolding her handkerchief.

'Cork city is a big place, but we will keep on the alert for him in that area.' Sergeant Kilroy pointed to the map. 'Why do you not believe what Finbar wrote in the note he left under his pillow, Mrs Kennedy? Let's have another look at the page in question.' The sergeant rummaged in a drawer, took out a large brown envelope with 'Missing Person' printed on the front, and written below it: Finbar Kennedy (born 1902) of 1 Park Terrace, Queenstown, The Cove of Cork.

'Of course I believe poor Finbar's little note, but I don't think he'd have the courage to run away to sea. My friend, Mrs Kelly, agrees. It is just his way of writing down some dream or something. Finbar is such a good boy, but he's a dreamer. Anyway, my husband, Jack, would have sent us word if Finbar was on board, and we've heard nothing. The whole idea is ridiculous, Sergeant.' She blew her nose. 'I don't want to get Jack into trouble either. We need his job. I'm sure Finbar will come home with his schoolbag some afternoon soon. Sure, Cork city is full of wonders for a young lad.' She looked at Colleen, who nodded.

'The note says,' the Sergeant looked at the children for a few moments and then turned towards Mam: '*Dear Mam, don't kill me, but I am sorry. I must go away to sea in a liner. Do not worry, people who know Dad will help me. And Dad will help me too when I tell him I ran away to sea to warn him about what I saw in my dreams. Then I will be home in a few days. Here are some pennies to buy eggs. I love you, and Colleen and Christopher and Sean. Your loving son, Finbar.*'

A young policeman came into the office and handed the Sergeant a note. The sergeant nodded and said, 'Will you ask your children to wait outside with one of the other officers, please, Mrs Kennedy?'

Mam stared at Colleen, who then put a hand on the neck of each of her brothers and led them outside. Mam shut the door and sat down again, facing Sergeant Kilroy.

'I went to Admiral Coke at the American Consulate last evening.' Sergeant Kilroy spoke slowly. 'The Admiral had the means of getting a message to your husband's ship. The American Consulate received a reply and passed it on to the barracks this morning. Will I read it to you, Mrs Kennedy?'

'Did they find Finbar? Is he in trouble? Is my husband in trouble? Finbar is the apple of his father's eye! The eldest son, you know ...' She put her face in her hands and began to moan.

'There now.' Sergeant Kilroy moved in his high-backed chair and adjusted the tunic around his neck uneasily. 'This is what the message says: "*RMS Lusitania 28 April 1915, received inquiry stop none by name of Finbar Kennedy boy aged thirteen en route to New York stop not on passenger or crew list stop.*' He folded the sheet of paper solemnly.

'Is that all?' begged Mam.

'I have read every word,' said the Sergeant. 'I assure you, Mrs Kennedy, we will continue to work on Finbar's case, and collect every scrap of information that comes our way, until we find him.'

'Oh well,' muttered Mam, getting up slowly, 'thank you, Sergeant.' She looked as if she were about to say something else, but instead she turned and went out of the room to her children, who huddled around her. 'Let's go home and have our supper, my pets. We'll call on Mrs Kelly and see if she has some nice treats.' She smiled sadly at their frightened faces, and none of them dared ask anything more about Finbar for the rest of the evening and the night.

CHAPTER 11

THE STOWAWAY

I felt small in the baggage storeroom among the boxes. My bones hurt. So did my chest and my back. My hands trembled. Sweat poured through my clothes. The desk was too hard to sleep on and the ledger and schoolbag were not the softest of pillows, but the gabardine coat was enough of a blanket because I was burning hot. I hoped I wouldn't fall off again. My breeches, long socks and boots were steaming and stuck to my body. I was really uncomfortable and even when the rat passed by me, searching for parcels to scratch open looking for food, I was beyond caring. Breathing hurt me. Sometimes I felt as if I might choke.

Time passed, how much time I did not know. Then I was woken in terror by someone pulling at my shirt. Was it the rat? A man's face was peering at me angrily. For a moment I thought it was Crowley, but it wasn't. The man held a lantern. He shouted: 'Who are you? What are you doing here, you waster?' His uniform was a bit like my father's. He grabbed hold of my shirt, pulled me off the desk roughly and shouted: 'I need to see your ticket. Your ticket for cargo class!'

He dragged me to the door. I pleaded with him for my schoolbag, the cap and the coat. 'Your ticket fell into the sea, I suppose? Yes, I know that story. We have cages for you people. Got no money, huh? Couldn't buy a lousy ticket. We might even feed you to the whales.' He snuffed out the lantern and dragged me out of the baggage room, closing the steel door with a vicious slam.

The lights on the walls outside made me squint as my eyes hurt from the glare. He pulled me along and I kept missing every other footstep, stumbling along the corridor. He opened a steel door at the end of the corridor and a stoker came out with a coal-stained face, holding a jug that he gulped from.

'Well, isn't he a puny herring!' he commented, pointing a sooty finger at me. 'Bad boy, what have you done, eh?'

'He's a millionaire on his way to America who lost his ticket,' answered the baggage steward. 'A gale blew up and took his ticket out to sea!'

'Cast him in irons!' said the stoker, and he laughed.

We came to a staircase and the man did not stop. My arm was nearly twisted out of its socket. My legs were sore from hitting against each other. I was dizzy. He kept hold of me with one arm as we mounted steps, and up four or maybe five flights of stairs. He stopped then and pushed me against the wall beside a door that had a round porthole window, with a gauze curtain showing some light from inside. He knocked, and as the door opened I noticed the word 'officers' painted in red below the window. The baggage man whispered something to the officer, who was reading charts.

The officer gave a quick look at me. 'You can go,' he said to the one who had dragged me in. 'What's 'is name? Where's he from? Liverpool, I suppose?'

'I dunno,' the baggage steward shook his head and left.

The officers' quarters were much finer than the horrible cargo place. For a moment I felt I was saved, but then I began to shiver with worry and a sickness that made me want to keel over. I realised also that the liner moved about more on this top deck. Out through a window I saw one of the chimney stacks, the white-painted decking, lifeboats, and, best of all, the sea going on for miles and miles to the horizon in the afternoon drizzle. My eyes watered and stung a little, seeing the wondrous sight. I gaped in awe and amazement at the swell of waves and the whole sky teeming with rain over it all.

'I'm officer John Lewis,' the man said in a gruff tone. He was a small, sturdy man with a moustache and large, bulging eyes. 'You must consider yourself under the jurisdiction of the officers and crew. We will hand you over to the police in New York.' His tone grew more severe. 'You will work in the stores for your food during the remainder of the voyage. If you cause any trouble, like fighting or stealing, you will be put in the cages. Is that understood? Why are you shivering, boy? Are you ill or something? Looks like you got the plague – the last bloody thing we need aboard a passenger liner!' He stared at me. 'What's your name, boy?' he asked, sitting down at a desk on which were pens, an ink well, Cunard headed notepaper, envelopes, maps and other documents.

'I'm Finbar Kennedy from Queenstown,' I managed to say as sweat poured down my face. Then, more brazenly, 'My father is Jack Kennedy. He is Staff Captain on the *Lusitania*.'

'Eh, you're Irish and you know what liner you are on.' He placed his hands flat on the desk. 'Who did you say your father is?' He stared at me as another officer came in, shaking the rain off.

'Got some company, John?' The tall officer had to stoop to come in the door.

'Got me a stowaway found in cargo,' replied Lewis at the desk. 'He claims Jack Kennedy is his father!'

'Oh and let me introduce myself,' said the tall man in mock formality. 'I am Officer Albert Bestic, and this is my fellow officer, John Lewis.' They both laughed.

'Take him down to the stores. He can run errands,' said Bestic.

'Please sir,' I begged Officer Bestic. 'Would someone fetch my father?'

The officers howled with laughter.

'He'll be wanting his mother next,' said Lewis. Then he lowered his voice. 'He does look like a sick calf though.'

'The Staff Captain,' said Bestic, 'should be in the wheelhouse with Captain Turner. What you say I go and get Jack Kennedy, clear up the situation and then take the boy to the stores where he can really work up a sweat! Keep him here until I get back.' Bestic opened the door, tilted his head and went out, letting it slam shut after him.

After a long time, Officer Bestic returned with Dad, who was holding papers and documents that he pushed into Bestic's hands when he saw me. He looked shocked, and his mouth opened as he tried to speak. I started to whimper and he ran over to me and put a hand on my forehead. Dad looked different than when he was at home. In fact, he looked as mean as Lewis and Bestic; the three of them were almost like brutes. I was too weak to tell him what had happened – how I'd run away, about the Baroness, the guns, the cane that nearly shot me, the secret talk about the German codebook as well as being locked in the cargo deck.

'Dad,' I muttered feebly, 'it's great to see you. I feel sick.'

Lewis, the shorter one, and Bestic, the taller one, suddenly looked kinder.

'Finbar, you have a fever,' Dad exclaimed. 'You look really bad. Albert, run for the medical officer. Tell him we have a very sick boy on board. This is my son Finbar. Tell Captain Turner I'll be delayed a while.' My father had Bestic hopping into action.

'Finbar, your Daddy will take care of you,' said Lewis, going to his desk, 'eh, Captain Kennedy?'

'John,' said my father sternly, 'write down every word I say and get it sent by telegraph immediately to Admiral Coke in

Queenstown.' Dad's voice was stern and official as he called out to Lewis, who wrote on a pad with a pencil: 'Attention Admiral Coke. Finbar Kennedy, son of Jack Kennedy, safely aboard the *Lusitania* today, 30 April 1915. Inform R.I.C. Queenstown and Mrs Kennedy & Family, 1 Park Terrace. All well on the high seas. John Kennedy, Staff Captain RMS *Lusitania*.'

'John, this is for immediate transmission. Okay?'

'Yes, Captain,' said Lewis, putting his peaked cap on quickly as he rushed out with the telegraph message.

Dad opened a cupboard from which he took a heavy blanket and wrapped it around me like a cloak. He lifted me on to a big chair that had two wooden arm rests. 'You got on board at Queenstown, and fell asleep?' He waited for an answer and bit his lip. Then he began to grin. 'Actually, I am secretly chuffed you are aboard the *Lusitania*, and once your mam knows you're safe … So, you jumped ship! What an adventurer we have!' My father's voice was beginning to break into a laugh and his face was beaming.

'Daddy, I'm sorry for the trouble I've caused.' My chest heaved and I started to sob, cough, and splutter.

'Well now, my son, I'm glad to see you safe and sound. But we must get you well.' He began to fix the blanket around my chest and then flung his arms around me. 'Wait until you see New York, son. I'll bet that's why you ran away.' He laughed and looked out into the dusk of the afternoon across the grey-blue mountainous waves of the sea. Then he felt my forehead. 'Cripes, you're burning up, boy, and you're shivering,' he said, staring at me with a worried look.

My father hoisted me over one shoulder and we headed out of the officer's quarters. The floors and walls moved past me as the liner swayed and heaved. Dad scrambled along and finally stopped at two white doors with a red cross on each. He put me down, took my hand and we walked into the ship's hospital.

CHAPTER 12

SEA HOSPITAL

'Captain Kennedy!' A man in a white coat, wearing spectacles, greeted Dad and looked down at me. 'So, this is your son. I heard about the situation from Officer Lewis. Follow me.'

'This is the medical officer, Doctor McDermott, and he will look after you,' Dad told me as we walked behind the doctor into a room divided into compartments. From midway up to the top of the ceiling the walls had glass panelling. Through bleary eyes I saw beds, tables, and cabinets containing bottles, small boxes, jars and silver medical instruments in glass jugs and beakers. Dad put me sitting on a bed and looked at Dr McDermott.

'Finbar has been in the stern cargo deck since we left

Queenstown.' Dad gave the doctor the details, but he didn't know the full story and I was too exhausted to tell them everything.

'Show me your tongue,' the doctor said, and examined me. I started to cough. 'Say Ah,' he said, and looked down my throat. 'Is your chest hurting?' I nodded. 'Breathe on to this.' He put a mirror in front of my mouth and my breath made it cloudy. He placed a glass thermometer under one of my arms and held it there.

'Did you eat or drink anything since coming aboard?' he asked. I shook my head and he gave me a puzzled look.

'Well, I drank the water off the walls in cargo because there was nothing else …' I said, remembering that awful time.

'Ah! I know what it is now, Finbar.' Dr McDermott clicked his fingers. 'It used to be a very common problem in the last century.' He turned to my father.

'Your son,' the doctor said, 'has a particular type of pneumonia. The water he took is unsuitable for drinking and it has infected his lungs with a nasty virus. His temperature is very, very high. We have to bring the temperature down.' He went out into a small corridor and called the ship's nurse, Nurse Ellis. 'I think we should keep him away from the others in the main ward.'

Dr McDermott opened a cupboard where there was a shelf with test tubes. He took down a jar of red powder and put a spoonful of it in one of the test tubes. He lit a candle in a holder and held the test tube above the flame. Soon the powder changed colour, the glass turned black from the flame and he asked me to inhale the smoky vapour streaming out of the test tube. 'That will help you breathe more easily,' he said, checking my pulse again.

'Poor boy,' said Nurse Ellis. She had thick, plaited hair and a white cap pinned on her head. She got pillows to prop me up, so I was soon snug except for my aches, pains and sweating. 'Isn't this a strange hospital, a sea hospital?' she said, smiling, but I was too sick to smile back. She rubbed my face with a sponge that smelt of some substance that reminded me of the peppermint drops and clove rock in Mrs Fitz's shop in Queenstown, though stronger.

'Dad,' I called, and he was waiting, fidgeting with his peaked cap. 'There's a man on the liner with a suitcase full of guns. He is a friend of the Baroness. His name is Mr...' suddenly with the fever and all I couldn't remember the name.

My father's brow was lined and furrowed as he listened.

'Then the Baroness ... what's her name, she has a codebook for sinking battleships. She is a German. The man is British...'

I was telling him all I could remember. 'Oh yes, and the man has a walking stick and it can fire a bullet and it did fire a bullet and nearly killed me…' I felt pleased that I could tell Dad what happened.

'Finbar is really not well at all,' Dad said to the doctor and Nurse Ellis. 'He's raving. Is this part of the illness too?'

'Your son is delirious, Captain,' said Dr McDermott – and the word *delirious* seemed to echo in my ears as if the doctor was saying it over and over. 'He is best left to our care.'

I just wanted to float off to sleep. My father, the nurse and the doctor became a blur before my eyes.

'I can see that,' said my father, 'but you understand the international situation with the war. I am duty-bound to check any piece of information from anyone to do with security. Just let me ask him one question before I go.'

'Very well, Captain. Then we'll let him sleep. He's your son, but it's my responsibility to restore his health.' The doctor sighed and folded his arms.

'Finbar, you definitely saw guns in a suitcase, did you? Where?'

I nodded, but sleep was slowly and safely leading me into its beautiful and peaceful world.

'In the cabin number…' I mumbled, but could not

remember the number of the Baroness's cabin. The room began to move in a swirl and fade away as my senses entered the healing halls of sleep.

Being sick is like being in a strange country, and being sick at sea with a fever was like being on another planet where I was a watery, wobbly creature made entirely of jelly, and where people's heads looked bigger, their voices echoed as if they talked to me from the bottom of a well, and I never knew if they heard what I said to them. They answered my questions as if I had asked something strange or had spoken in a language they did not understand.

I lost track of time. Night and day were the same. Nurse Ellis was so good; she was always there. She showed me a little card with my name 'Finbar Kennedy' written on it and underneath, in red ink, the letters: 'VP'. 'That means Viral Pneumonia,' she explained.

'Are they the code words for my name?' I asked her. 'Are you a spy?' She went for Dr McDermott, who came and looked at me, his long face looking serious.

'Nurse, you must try and get him to eat as he's so weak.' His voice was like an echo.

The gaslamp in the corner above the bed was too bright when I stared at it for long. I dozed off, I woke up, I dozed off again. Sometimes I thought I was in Queenstown and expected to see Mam, Colleen, Christopher and Sean.

Sometimes when I woke up Dad was sitting beside me on the bed. 'There is no school on the *Lusitania,* you'll be glad to hear,' he said one day. He had brought my clothes, my cap, the schoolbag and handed me the five dollars he'd found in my pocket that the Baroness had given me for carrying her suitcases. 'Your mother knows you're safe. They got our message. Captain Turner is asking after you. In two days we will be docking in New York,' he announced.

I was about to try to tell him again about the guns, but he stood up, put his hand to my forehead, and said, 'Get well, shipmate.' He was in a hurry to get away to his work. 'We can talk when you're fully recovered,' he said.

I was given hot lemon with crushed garlic to drink, which was very hard to swallow because it burned my throat. I sweated. I tossed and turned like the liner. Nurse Ellis brought chicken broth with chopped onions in it. And after one spoonful I began to feel that my throat was not so sore.

Then one day I woke up and heard no sound on the liner.

The engines had stopped. I was certain of that because it was so still and the boat did not move around. My aches and pains had gone and the sweats had disappeared, my forehead and temples were cool, and my chest heaved up and down gently.

Nurse Ellis breezed in and I heard her voice clearly, as if for the first time. She held my wrist, looked at her watch and counted the beats of my pulse. 'You're over it,' she announced. 'I think you should walk a bit,' she suggested, and helped me into my clothes that had been washed clean and fresh. My schoolbag looked odd so far away from home. I looked inside and smiled when I saw my penknife, the conker and the wooden liner.

'Has the *Lusitania* stopped?' I asked. My legs were a bit shaky when I walked. For the first time I could see the liner's hospital clearly. My room opened on to a bigger room with rows of beds on each side. There were small tables between the beds and there were curtains on rails around the beds. There were no other patients.

'We docked just after eleven this morning,' said Nurse Ellis. 'It is now four o'clock in the afternoon. Your father will collect you in the Cunard office. We must hurry, now. It's across the wharf. Pier 54, on 14th Street. We mustn't miss him. Let's go up to the sun deck and give you your first sight of New York.'

She led the way with a big grin, and I followed her up two flights of stairs.

'Look,' Nurse Ellis said in a loud voice, 'you'll need your legs today – and you will have to walk better than a newborn foal. Look over there. Look!' She was quite excited herself. 'You are in America.' She hugged me and I thought she was about to cry. I could have cried too. God, had this nurse been good to me! She was like my mother at sea.

Amid the Skyscrapers of New York

CHAPTER 13

WHAT A CITY!

I stared in awe at what met my eyes as we came out of the stairwell and through a steel door on to the sun deck of the *Lusitania* – huge buildings like castles, and towers of incredible shapes, covered in windows that looked like millions of ladders with glass between the rungs, and reaching up to the sky. The buildings were taller than anything I had ever seen in my life and looked like an undiscovered world from a fantastic universe. They almost blotted out the sky. The buildings and towers went on as far as the eye could see. New York was massive. Everything was so big, it was a wonder that the people below on the dockside weren't all ten-foot giants.

The sun was shining and there was a sharp breeze off the harbour. Throngs of people moved about on the docks, where horse-drawn cabs stood in lines waiting for fares. Cranes were loading and unloading items of great bulk from the *Lusitania* and other liners.

Nurse Ellis tugged at my arm, leading me towards a gangplank high above the wharf, and together we walked down the slope. It was an unforgettable moment. I had run away on the *Lusitania*! I was in New York!

'Skyscrapers!' I laughed. 'I bet my teacher, Mr Dempsey, would like to write that word on his blackboard. Scraping the sky, he'd explain.' I laughed giddily.

'My, you must love school,' she said, 'to think of your teacher at a time like this. Come on, Finbar, I have to meet my sister. And you have to wait for your dad. He gave me some official papers for you, allowing you to get off here. Please mind them carefully.' We headed down the gangplank but a police officer wearing a gun and holster came over.

'Papers, please,' he said in an American accent. 'You are very late disembarking, ma'am. Have you permission to stay aboard so long?' He looked puzzled.

'We are crew members,' Nurse Ellis replied, showing him her ID, 'and this is Staff Captain Kennedy's son, Finbar.' She handed him more papers.

'Yes, ma'am.' The policeman stepped aside, handed her

back her papers and unhooked the chain at the end of the gangplank.

I still couldn't believe my eyes and didn't know where to look, everything was so new and exciting. Nurse Ellis gave me the official papers and said goodbye at the Cunard office; she kissed me on the cheek and we hugged. I thanked her for minding me and walked in the door of the office, feeling like a sailor who had travelled around the world!

'I am to wait here for my father, Captain Jack Kennedy,' I told the man at the desk, who wore a visor that was like a peak made of green cellophane across his forehead.

'Okay by me, bud,' he replied, and then he gave a foxy grin. 'You okay, kid? You sit on the bench there. Your pop will be along soon. Okay?'

Later, my father entered with other men in uniform. He waved to me and smiled for a moment. I stayed sitting while he talked with the others. They all did a lot of nodding and fixing of their caps, scratched their faces and those who had beards, like him, tugged at them. I lost interest and stared out through the windows and realised that the *Lusitania* was a mighty liner and that I truly loved it.

Dad came over and broke in on my trance. He beckoned me to pick up my schoolbag and follow him outside. 'You look like the real Finbar Kennedy now, not that ghost we found on the *Lusitania*,' he said, and stroked his beard in silence. I wondered if he was going to talk about my running away from home. 'Listen, I have to tell you secret information – well, as much as I am allowed. You must tell no one what happened to you on the ship. No one. We don't want to scare people away. That is very important.'

I nodded in amazement as he led me away from the Cunard office to an empty space with stacks of wooden crates and barrels marked 'Crude American Oil'. Our view as we talked was of a busy crossway of four streets with a signpost for 14th Street and another sign above that, in blue, that said Pier 54.

'Now,' he said, 'this is serious. Can you remember the name of the man you saw with the suitcase full of guns? He was the man with the cane that shot a bullet into one of the walls of Cabin 13 and broke the mirror, remember?' He had obviously followed up on my story. He looked at me expectantly.

'I can't remember his name, Dad,' I replied. 'He was a bald man. Tall. I was in the cabin because the Baroness had got me to lift her luggage. I had to escape and in the struggle there was a shot. Honestly.' I knew by his solemn look that he believed me now. He folded his arms and listened carefully to everything that had happened to me up to my time in the hospital. It was a long story. I had tried to tell him some of it when I was sick, but he didn't seem to understand me because of the fever. Now, here in New York, on the docks, he listened to it all and was amazed.

'You see, Finbar,' Dad began after I had talked for a long time, 'we had a complaint during the voyage that someone heard a shot. We tracked it to Baroness Leonie von Leiditz in Cabin 13. She, of course, said there was no shot. But it all tied in with what I thought were your delusions. Now, is Aleister Crowley the name of the man who had the suitcase full of guns?'

'Yes! That's it! Crowley is the name. I remember now.'

Dad pushed his hat back on his head and took out a sheet of paper from his inside pocket. 'Some of our cabin staff saw Crowley with Baroness von Leiditz and identified him for me.' He read from the paper. 'His full name is Edward Alexander Crowley. He's British. He is a famous writer, a mysterious man – and obviously dealing in arms – but he denied everything as he hurried off the liner into a taxi this morning with a lot of heavy luggage, including the guns, I'd bet. But we can't search a passenger's luggage unless we have the police to supervise the situation,' Dad explained. He was speaking low and in a voice I had never heard before.

'You were in great danger when you met that man, Finbar.

It is so lucky that you escaped his clutches.' His tone was serious and he was talking to me as if I were another staff captain. 'If by any chance you see him here in New York, get away from him immediately.'

I felt like a player in a big game all of a sudden. This was life and it was more exciting than school or anything that had happened to me up to now. But it was dangerous too.

'I read an article about Crowley in the *New York Times*,' he continued. 'It said that he is a self-publicist and a propagandist. But he's involved in shady things like gun-running too.' Dad wiped his mouth slowly.

I was beginning to get anxious, but also hoping Dad would not stop telling me the details. 'Is he going to kill someone?' I tried to sound like an adult – after crossing the Atlantic on the *Lusitania*, I felt really grown up.

'Crowley writes for a newspaper called *The Fatherland*, which is pro-German; in other words, it boosts German morale during the war and deliberately prints news that is anti-British. He even makes up lies to try to turn people against Britain. The newspaper can be published in America because America is not in the Great War. America is neutral, do you get it?'

'Not really, Dad,' I said.

'Well, son, Britain and Germany spy on each other because they are at war. Crowley, as a British citizen, is up to no good mixing with a wealthy German Baroness, especially when they are enemies. British politicians treat Crowley as a crank or a kind of fool because he writes anything for any newspaper or magazine that pays him, but they largely ignore him. The man has no principles, no sense of what's right and what's wrong. But he's no fool either.' Dad exhaled loudly and looked at me. He had me scared now. His eyes were cold and he seemed to be far off in his thoughts. 'He's big trouble, and I'll be glad to leave all that behind on our return journey. We wouldn't want the likes of him on board again. He's a really dangerous type.'

Dad looked up and down the street, then at our luggage – his navy sack and my schoolbag. He picked up the sack, handed me the schoolbag and we turned to enter the omnibus station where there were lots of big buses and long queues.

'Finbar, the world is at war,' Dad said. 'We're in danger because of being on the *Lusitania*. You didn't realise what a big step you took hiding on board the *Lusitania*! Our ship needs to be protected by Royal Navy battleships when we're at sea. The Atlantic Ocean is enemy territory. Get it now?'

But I decided to forget about the danger for a while. I was in America with my Dad. It was a great adventure.

CHAPTER 14

NEW YORK COMFORTS

O ur three days in New York passed like lightning and were full of new experiences. That very first day Dad and I bought two hotdogs from a stall in the omnibus station, and ate them savagely because we were starving. Then we joined the queue for the bus. We had huge grins on our faces as we sat at the front where we had a good view of everyone passing up and down the streets.

'We are on Manhattan island, son,' said Dad. 'The avenues are north to south,' he explained, 'and the streets east to west.'

'It's called "man-hat-on",' I joked because the scene made me feel cheeky and both of us had our caps on, his peaked naval one and my school cap.

We got out and walked past a sign for 16th Street. At No.

132 was Ward's Rooming House and we went up the steps there and in through double doors. Dad rang the bell at the desk and a woman came out through beads on cords that rattled as she moved.

'Well hello, Captain Jack,' she said. Her hair was tied up on her head with what looked to me like small sticks, and she wore spectacles. 'Oh wow, you brought one of your sons! He looks really like you.' The woman had big white shining teeth that filled her smiling face. 'Going to sea at a young age, eh?' she said to me. 'Aren't you the brave lad!' She caught me by the ear, tugging at it until I began to laugh loudly.

'This is my son Finbar. This is Josephine Weir,' Dad introduced us.

'Well, I am mighty glad to meet you, Finbar,' said Josephine. 'How long are you staying this time?' she asked Dad.

'Three nights.' Dad signed the book. 'How is everything in Weir's famous rooming house?'

'Tonight I'm getting out of here to go bowling – and leaving the others get on with the work.' She lit a cigarette and blew smoke out of her mouth in a little cloud. 'I bet Finbar would like a hot tub.' Josephine came from behind the desk and put her hand around my shoulder in a hug. 'What a fine boy, and a handsome boy too.' She grinned, showing her pearly teeth again. 'You sailors can dump your luggage in the locker behind the desk, go get a hot tub and come back later. Your luggage will be brought to your room – it's on the seventh floor, I'm afraid, as we're almost booked out. April is kinda the start of the summer season, you know.' She exhaled smoke again, talking between drags of the cigarette. We pushed the luggage into the locker.

Before we left the hostel Dad had a piece of advice for me. 'If you get lost in the next few days, son, find an Irish cop and he'll show you the way to Weir's place.' Then he tweaked me on the nose. 'Hey, after what you've done you won't get lost, will you? You're thirteen, now – let's hope it's a lucky year for you, Finbar.'

We set out for Bowery Bath House where at the entrance were lots of shops, cafés, laundries for washing clothes, barber's shops and bars. Beyond, in the corridors, people filed along in bathrobes in their bare feet, with wet hair, the women and girls down one corridor, the men and boys along another. The corridors were so wide and high they looked like streets. I got a cubicle number and Dad got one too, and we changed into our bathrobes. My cubicle had a door that led into a small, steamy compartment where there was a big bath. The taps were wheels on the wall and a chunk of soap was wedged onto a piece of wood on a rough chain. There was also a bath brush on a chain. The bath itself was deep with steps up to it and a wooden seat below the water. I sat down and the water came up to my neck. I rubbed the brush hard along my back and neck, giving myself a bracing scrub. Dad was singing in the cubicle next door, so I joined in a chorus of 'The Banks of My Own Lovely Lee'. When he sang 'Skibbereen' other voices mingled with his and the whole bellowing concert made me laugh madly as the hot water, steam and soap cleaned me thoroughly.

'Finbar, are you cooked?' shouted Dad, banging on the door. 'Are you turning into a seal in there?'

'I'm ready,' I shouted.

Still in the bathhouse, we next went to the barber's. By the time we came out into the street our faces were glowing, and our hair was trimmed and parted, and glistening with oil.

Then Dad took me back to the front door of Weir's because he needed to visit the Cunard office in Upper Manhattan.

CHAPTER 15

CHINATOWN

During the days in New York I walked the streets, gazing at everything in amazement. There were millions of people in the city and the buildings cast long shadows, and on some streets it was dark and on others dazzlingly bright. You couldn't really see the sky because it hurt your neck looking up so far.

On our second night Dad took me to an amazing place. Even the street was different to every other street I had seen so far. The people were mostly Chinese. The buildings had archways at the entrance with lanterns and paper dragons; the shop fronts were mostly red and black, and many had incense smoking in lamps at the doors that caught my nose, making me sneeze. There was strange twanging music from harps, stringed instruments, bells and drums.

We went into a hotel in Chinatown where the staff wore black caps, had pigtails, and seemed to shuffle in and out slowly and with great ease and dignity no matter how busy they were. Dad ordered and we were served lots of tiny dishes of fish and meat, with brightly coloured sauces. He ate with chopsticks, but after a messy attempt, I stuck to a knife and fork.

Then a woman in a red cloak with coloured birds sewn onto it came over to our table. Her hair was as black as coal. She had white powder painted all over her face, except for red paint on her lips and black paint at her eyebrows. She smelt like flowers.

'I am Lily Lee.' She had a beaming smile. 'Can I tell your son's fortune, sir? One dollar – a really special deal for the boy.' She smiled and bowed.

'You go ahead,' Dad said, and he peeled off a note from his wedge, telling me to hold onto my eleven dollars.

'Give me your hand,' Lily Lee said as she sat on a chair near me. Her eyes became narrow. She gasped. Her eyes shone like jewels as she stared at me.

'Hey, this is a bit strange,' said Dad.

'Be patient, sir. Your son knows some things that you do

not.' Lily Lee became silent and motionless again. Then she breathed in loudly, closed her eyes and when they opened she stared into a vacant space above my head. 'Be careful, boy,' she said. 'I see you in grave danger on a ship. You want to see your sister and brothers again, don't you?'

'But how could you know he has a sister and brothers?' Dad was amazed.

But Lily Lee ignored him. 'You watch out, sonny,' she said slowly. 'In time of war a boy at the centre of bad things can survive. Remember that.' She repeated this three times, stared at my father as she bowed, moved backwards, facing us for a while, then rushed away and disappeared outside into the crowd of passersby.

Dad looked worried for a moment and then indicated that we were leaving. He paid the bill, left a tip and we walked outside. 'You all right?' he asked as we strolled along the sidewalk. 'You look as if you've seen a ghost.' He stopped and put one hand on my shoulder.

'Is she a witch or what?' I asked, a bit shaken. 'What did she mean?'

'Finbar, I don't know, but she has you scared, I can see that. Lily Lee saw that I was in naval uniform – that doesn't make her so gifted with second sight!'

'But, Dad,' I blurted out – somehow I got the courage to tell him – 'Dad, there's going to be a shipwreck. I saw it in a powerful dream.'

He said nothing at first, then he turned to me with glaring eyes. 'Let's get to bed, son. It's been a long day and sleep must be our next port of call.'

Next morning over breakfast he mentioned the dream and what I'd said. 'The problem is, Finbar, talk is dangerous. In New York, if you talk about a shipwreck that is going to happen you'll sound like a spy. There's evil in the air. You are picking up the signals in your dreams.' He paused, and looked at me seriously. 'On our return journey I'll fix you up with a job as a messenger on board ship, but you can also act as a spy for me, and, like a spy, you must tell no one what you discover, except Captain Turner and myself.' Dad tapped me on the shoulder and smiled.

'But I ran away from home b-b–because I wanted to protect you from danger.'

'I understand, son,' Dad said. 'And now you can help protect us all from danger on our home journey.'

My mood changed to one of steely courage. 'Dad, I'll do my best. But I can't wait till we're home in Queenstown.'

CHAPTER 16

THE GREAT WARNING

The following morning was Sunday, the day of our departure, and my father had to shake me awake because I was so tired after a late Saturday night in the Mayflower restaurant with the rest of the *Lusitania* crew. I proudly put on my new uniform and cap. My schoolbag was under the bed, but school was so far away across the world, it seemed as if it had all ended and Mr Dempsey had vanished. With a wide grin, I stuffed my schoolbag and school cap into my new knapsack. How could I leave them behind? Dad paid our bill and Josephine Weir gave us a big, cheery goodbye.

'Will you get a newspaper,' Dad said and handed me a coin on our way past a big Port Authority sign. I rushed along the sidewalk, pushed the coin into the slot that opened the newspaper rack from which I took a copy. I could have taken two copies or more, but in New York they trusted you to take only what you'd paid for. The *New York Times* was folded in two. The date below the title was 1 May 1915. My reading skills, thanks to Mr Dempsey, were fairly good, still I went through the paper looking only at the pictures of the war in Europe – at aeroplanes, artillery, buildings destroyed by bombing and soldiers in trenches with their rifles and bayonets wearing gasmasks, making them look scary. Then I noticed an advertisement for the *Lusitania*: 'Sail to Europe on the World's Fastest and Safest Transatlantic Liner; *Four Sailings per Month*'. There were times and dates for sailings, and prices for first, second and third class tickets. Then I saw another advertisement in a thick, black border. I read it slowly and had to stand still, it scared me so much:

NOTICE

Attention travellers on the Atlantic Ocean, bound for Great Britain and Ireland. You travellers will enter the war zone when you approach the West and South Coast of Ireland. All vessels in these waters flying the flag of our enemies are liable to destruction. Know ye that we will fire upon such liners in the waters of the war zone.

I nearly dropped the newspaper, hardly hearing the noise in

the street anymore. I saw Dad coming along with officers John Lewis and Albert Bestic. Both smiled when they recognised me.

'So, our stowaway has got his shipping papers this time,' Bestic teased.

'Dad—'

'Come on, Finbar, we're late.' Dad rushed ahead.

Soon we were in a horse-drawn taxi with leather seats, a door on each side, and windows. I could see the driver through a small oval window up front, holding a whip. I said nothing on the journey while the men chatted loudly. We were dropped off at Pier 54.

The pier was crowded with people, automobiles, taxicabs like the one I had been in, and crewmen with carts full of luggage. There was a three-man band, dressed in green suits and green bowler hats, entertaining the arriving passengers, playing 'My Irish Molly-O' and other tunes on the accordion, fiddle and banjo. The *Lusitania* had jets of smoke coming from its four chimneystacks and its flagmasts rose grandly up into the sky. Dad shoved the *New York Times* into his luggage. When would he see the notice? What would he say?

Dad beckoned me to follow him as he walked along the dock through the teeming passengers who jostled each other, awaiting permission from the liner's stewards to board the vessel. I noticed many people reading the *New York Times* and wondered if they had seen the notice. Out on the dockside, cranes hoisted food in crates marked: eggs, bread, fish, fruit, vegetables. Four vast, long gangways sloped from the liner's lowest deck to the dock. Dad walked up one of the gangplanks, past crewmen with brass buttons on their tunics and wearing flat caps. They were hauling the remaining cargo of sackfuls of letters and packages on board, using a deck crane. We went up the stairs to the upper deck. The liner hummed and throbbed underneath us.

Along the top deck, children played games of chasing, while others were skipping and rolling hoops, and some hopped on the hopscotch area where numbers and squares were painted on the floor.

'Are you the Captain?' asked a little boy in a sailor suit.

'I'm the Staff Captain,' Dad replied. 'And this is my son.'

'Our father is the United States Senator, Richard Mayberry,' said a taller girl, who was the boy's sister. She had blond hair with a fringe, and sounded as if she were going to make a speech. She wore a blue blazer, white pinafore and thin, white woollen stockings. Her shiny black patent shoes had silver clasps. 'I am Penny Mayberry and this is my brother John. He is eight.' She spoke very politely and formally. I was unable to speak, staring as her large eyes focused on mine. For some reason I bowed as if she were a princess. Her refined American accent and her bright smile shook me for a moment so that my surroundings seemed to disappear. 'And what is your name, young man?' she asked me.

'My name is F–F–Finbar,' I stuttered, fixing my cap straight. She smiled warmly and raised the palm of one hand, making a circle in the air in a kind of wave.

'We must go, we are on duty. Goodbye, children,' said Dad, and we went up two further sets of stairs towards a gateway with a red sign saying: NO ENTRY, CREW ONLY. Dad took out a key and let us in. We climbed steps to the bridge with its steel wall of square windows looking into the wheelhouse. Dad told me that this was the main hub of the thirty-thousand-ton turbine driven liner. 'Under full steam, the turbine propellers produce 68,000 horse power and make a speed of twenty-five knots,' he explained. His tone had become official and somehow I knew that any intimate conversation would have to cease now that he was at work. He told me to wait inside the door while he went to attend to things and I stood there on a mat made from thick rope. Two men in uniform had their backs to me; one wrote in a notebook while the other looked at dials and gauges before writing numbers on a page in a clipboard. Another man tended the wheel with its handles and brass edgings. There was an indicator with words in black on the white metal signs: AHEAD, ASTERN, SLOW and a thick needle pointing to FULL.

Captain Turner turned around when one of the officers spoke to him and nodded solemnly. He squared up his cap and walked past the dials and instruments section of the bridge. For a moment, he twirled a button of his double-breasted, navy-blue blazer and mounted the stairs to the wheel-room from where the liner was steered. I had never seen such an amazing place and being up so high in the liner made me feel immense power.

'Captain Kennedy, check the passenger list and the cargo list please, and get the latest weather reports.' Captain Turner stood tall, like my father. His cap had braid on the peak. He held a hard-covered file marked *The Log of the Lusitania*. I waited, looked around and noticed how, far below us, the people on the pier looked tiny.

Dad called me over and just as I was about to tell him about the notice in the *Times*, he pointed to VIP written after some names on the list. 'That means Very Important Person,' he informed me. 'Mrs Mabel Mayberry, the wife of Senator

Richard Mayberry, is accompanied by her children, Penelope and John. Rita Jolivet is a Hollywood actress. Sir Hugh Lane is an international art dealer.' There were many names on the pages.

'The American VIPs are millionaires,' Dad said, and moved his thumb down the long list. 'Let's go and check the cargo.'

I followed him outside, feeling confused. 'Dad, there's a notice in the *New York Times*,' I finally blurted out. When I told him what the notice said he rushed back into the wheelhouse to tell Captain Turner. At last I could relax. They would read the notice saying that the Germans considered the Atlantic Ocean a war zone. They would know what to do.

CHAPTER 17

SECRET CARGO

s Dad's first tour of duty began, he told me to follow him. He said nothing while we walked along corridors and descended staircases, through many doors that slammed behind us, until we stood on a steel platform with railings that led down into the centre of the liner where the noise increased. This cargo deck had the widest corridors and doors that creaked open into a vast area, where I couldn't see the other end since it went on and on out of sight. A crewman approached Dad and they talked for a few moments. Then Dad walked around piled stockades of cargo, shouting out the name of each lot as he checked them off in a notepad: bales of leather, automobile parts, dental goods, crates of books, sewing machines, oil paintings, wool, aluminium, steel and bronze powder.

He turned a corner and told me to stay behind and not to follow him. 'Nobody is permitted in here,' he said, looking at me very sternly. 'This is top secret.'

'Of course, Dad,' I said.

He disappeared for a few minutes, then returned, and we headed out.

'Strictly no smoking, Mister Smith,' he said to the crewman, who let us out and locked the door after us.

We soon returned to the passenger corridors with cabins, stairs and signs. After the dark cargo hold the galley seemed very bright with its portholes and lights. We sat at a table and a chef with a floppy white hat served us oxtail soup with bread rolls and butter, followed by fish, chips, and beans. 'You can have both desserts too, lad, if you can sink them,' he told me, and winked and tapped his large stomach with a fist.

'Dad, did you and Captain Turner read the *New York Times* warning notice?' I gulped down water, poured more ketchup on my chips and wiped my mouth.

'The notice in the newspaper was written by Aleister Crowley, but not for the *New York Times*, it was first published in *The Fatherland*, which is a German paper published in New York. Crowley is a spy and propagandist,' Dad explained. 'He is a writer willing to write anything for anybody for money.

He writes an awful lot of propaganda.'

'Dad, what's propaganda?' I asked.

'It's often lies or half-truths. I told you about it before, remember? It is meant to force people to change their views, especially about the war. It frightens people. So if, for example, a person supports the British in this war, propaganda is used to try to get them to support the Germans instead. This is done by threatening them.'

'Like frightening them off the *Lusitania*?'

'Yes, that sort of thing. If they're scared to take the ship, then the business stops. I think the more people who see the warning notice, the better – there will be some passengers who'll get scared, of course, but it's better if everyone is alert.'

'Will the ship be attacked, Dad?'

'We run the *Lusitania*, Finbar, and we run a good ship. It's the fastest ship anywhere. We aim to get safely across the Atlantic.' Dad smiled proudly. 'You know your duties, Finbar: cabin service, running errands and, most important of all, keeping alert for anything suspicious among the passengers.' He put a finger to his forehead and saluted.

'Okay, Dad. You can trust me.' My spoon was loaded with my last chunk of hot apple pie and custard. 'This is a great liner.'

Dad rubbed his hands together and stood up. 'You better get to McCormick in the Marconi room and get the weather charts. It's on the top deck – the sun deck – between the second and third chimney stacks.'

I made my way out onto the top deck, past the two funnels and arrived at the Marconi radio room. A man in a shirt and naval trousers let me in when I knocked. He had two messages written out beside the Morse Code apparatus on top of a sloping desk where there were lots of notepads and pencils. A sign on the wall said: *Attention: Telegrams 6 Cents Per Word Payable before Transmission. No Refunds.* The Morse Code apparatus was a tiny hammer on a hinge above a screwtop. There were wires attached to the apparatus that picked up signals from any other Morse Code apparatus within range. Suddenly, as I looked, the hammer began to hit the screwtop with long and short pauses between taps, and the operator bade me be silent as he listened and wrote out two lines of words in pencil.

'Are you Mister McCormick?' I asked when he had finished. 'I have to collect the weather charts for the bridge.'

'Here they are,' he said. He rustled through charts on a desk behind him and rolled up two of them into cylinders. He turned away from me then as the apparatus began tapping out another message.

I decided to take a short cut through the corridor past the first class cabins. As I descended the staircase carefully so as not to fall or drop the charts, Penny Mayberry and her brother John waved at me to come over to them.

'Can you walk with us?' Penny noticed the rolled-up charts. 'I will soon be dropping John back to Mom. He was playing ball on deck.' She made a cross face to me, looking down at him. 'Mom is already seasick. Well, I mean, she was laid up with worry when she read the notice in the *New York Times*. My father, Senator Mayberry is always talking about the war…' she tucked some strands of blond hair behind one ear and a few of them brushed my shoulder as we moved away in the opposite direction from Crowley. Penny's eyes caught me in their gaze, making me forget my duty for a moment; they were green like the sea.

'Is Mom ill?' John asked his sister.

'No, John, she is resting so as not to get ill,' she explained and then looked at me. 'What are those papers you have?' She reminded me of the task in hand.

'Oh! Charts!' I stammered. 'I better be going immediately…'

I would have given anything to stay with her.

'Can I meet you later? I have to tell you something very important.' She grasped her brother's hand, dragging him along.

'I am off duty at nineteen hundred hours. Seven o'clock.' My sense of pride in my work made me sound very important, I thought.

'Let's see. I will meet you at seven in the games room.' She gave me a smile.

I ran off, feeling a strange sort of excitement.

CHAPTER 18

SAILING OUT OF NEW YORK

W hen I burst in the door of the wheelhouse Dad was looking out one of the windows on the bridge, facing the funnel that had slanting cables holding it in place. All four of the chimney funnels had similar cables along the full length of the liner towards the stern. I noticed the *New York Times* lying on the ledge beside the liner's wheel and it was folded in two, showing the page with the warning notice. They must have been discussing it, but nobody said anything to me about it.

I handed the charts to Officer Lewis, who took them without even glancing in my direction. He opened them up under a bright lamp on his desk and began studying them.

'The Kaiser and his Huns don't scare me, wasting their money on ten-cent-a-line propaganda in the *New York Times*,' Captain Turner announced to a man wearing a blue pinstripe suit and a bowler hat who was sitting on a chair next to the captain. 'Detective Inspector William Pierpoint, this is Captain Kennedy, Officer Lewis, and our youngest crewman, Finbar Kennedy,' said the captain. Dad shook hands with the detective who hardly looked at me. His face was pale and serious with dark patches around his eyes.

'What you call ten-cent propagandists, Captain Turner,' Detective Pierpoint said with a nasal American accent, 'I have to take seriously line by line. These ten-cent writers of propaganda threaten our lives since they make or break public opinion. Opinions printed in newspapers in time of war are just as dangerous as bombs.' He took a pipe out of his pocket and gestured with it as he spoke. 'Now I have an announcement to make,' he said. 'No one except high-ranking members of the crew must be allowed to send telegraph messages during the voyage in case anything is transmitted by Morse Code that might end up in the newspapers and draw attention good, bad or indifferent to the *Lusitania*. All passengers' telegrams will have to be checked by me in case they contain some coded message. All right if I smoke?' he held the pipe in the palm of one hand and stuffed it with tobacco, then lit a match, puffed on the stem and smoke soon encircled his face.

'Captain Turner, if you sign the cargo documents I will make ready to set sail.' Dad bristled with activity. 'We have received a report from the engine room. All good.'

'Everything is in order, then, Captain Kennedy?' Captain Turner too became more official as the moment for departure came closer. 'The weather is glorious for the start of May, almost a hint of summer.' He stared out towards the bow of the great liner and then up at the sky.

'We should sail out of New York without a ripple,' Dad said as he took measurements on a chart with his ruler and dividers.

'Well, I hope the voyage goes without a ripple.' Pierpoint pulled the pipe out of his mouth and poked at the bowl of it with a used match to stir up the fading tobacco flames.

'I have outrun many U-boats since the war began, Mr Pierpoint. Damn this threat of torpedoing the *Lusitania*! No one could catch our *Lucy*. She is the fastest of all the ships at sea.' Captain Turner spoke confidently as he looked through his binoculars. 'Besides,' Turner's voice suddenly frightened me,'we have hundreds of lifebelts and over a thousand to spare. And the thirty lifeboats can carry up to seventy passengers each. There are also twenty-six collapsible boats for the crew.'

'Detective Inspector, you will have to leave the wheelhouse now as we're ready to get under way. It's eleven-twenty, and we expect to cast off at eleven-forty. We trust you'll be taking care of any spy situation on board,' Dad said.

Pierpoint stood up. 'Let's talk tonight at dinner.'

Captain Turner nodded and began to examine one of the weather maps that I had delivered, smoothing down the edges with his hand. 'Finbar,' he bade me come forward with a gesture as he called out orders on the liner's tannoy system, 'take this to the chief engineer pronto.' He handed me a sealed yellow envelope marked: Engine Room. 'This is very important. Make sure it gets to him personally. Keep on the alert, Master Kennedy,' he warned, 'we are all working for a safe voyage.'

I saluted and he saluted in return. Dad was busy in another corner so I left, unable to ask directions to the engine room. I would find it myself. On the top deck I pushed the letter into my pants pocket, slung myself down the stairs the way sailors do – holding the rails, tipping off very few steps – and I landed a deck below. 'Where's the engine room?' I shouted to a steward carrying luggage, and he shouted out directions. I ran off.

Suddenly the liner came alive with vibrations. The vast engine room was divided by iron grating with gaslights flickering at different levels amidst the stir of powerful machinery. There was a smell of hot metal, the heat of burning coal and a mist of steam, making the atmosphere unbearably hot. Pressure clocks, fuel tanks and giant pistons were continually pumping, while the crewmen on a steel floor below me wore rough military clothes, goggles and helmets.

'Don't let the crew above deck fool you, son,' shouted one of the crewmen. He startled me with his coalblack face. 'We're the ones who really make this ship go. Without us, this liner will go nowhere.' He began telling me about the coalbunkers that held six thousand tons of Eureka coal. The persistent shattering noise made it difficult to hear all of what he said and I grew impatient, coming out in a sweat, and shouted back that I needed to see the 'chief engineer pronto', using Captain Turner's words. He directed me and returned to shovelling the loose lumps of coal that were everywhere as I headed off.

Fire-hoses, axes and crowbars were in open cupboards everywhere and there were many DANGER signs in black on a backdrop of red. Steam vapour and the deep smell of crackling, burning coal filled my nostrils. As I walked up a ladder towards a platform to reach the engineer's den I saw squads of firemen with sooty faces shovelling coal into the open furnace doors. The coal plopped in among the dancing flames and red-hot coals, while sheets of flame billowed out, licking the edges of the furnace doors, making the firemen recoil and wipe their brows. This was a scary place. Suddenly I wanted to scream at the immensity of the liner, the war, and not knowing what was going to happen.

The chief engineer took the yellow envelope that instantly turned into black soot in his hands as he pulled out the note from Captain Turner and read it quickly.

'Tell the Captain,' he scrunched the paper into a ball in his fist and bellowed into my face, spraying me with spittle, 'tell the Captain, we are ready for every emergency, come what may.'

His message scared me and I began to repeat it so I wouldn't get it wrong: 'Every emergency, come what may.'

I rushed up onto the top gallery and heard the boilers rumbling below with hundreds of gallons of scalding hot water in their innards. Slowly, the huge turbines began to turn the four mighty screws linked to the propellers in the stern that displaced water in the sea below the liner, making waves of foam. I was relieved to reach the top step of the last staircase in the engine room.

From the top deck, I saw that the liner was ready to set sail like some giant sea monster with four huge black tusks on its head. The chimneystack funnels belched out smoke and sparks as the smell of coal mingled with the fresh sea air in the harbour. Seagulls formed above the ship in clusters, shrieking and screaming. On the open deck and the top deck, known as 'the hurricane deck', passengers waved and shouted 'Goodbye', 'Happy days', 'See you soon' to people on the dock as the gangplanks were lowered. Trios of sailors twisted winches and the thick tow-ropes were wound slowly around the deck bollards as the anchors and ropes were hauled in.

The liner began to move like a huge, dark phantom. The eight-hundred-foot-long magnificent ship made a three-quarter turn in the water, showing the high rump of its stern, proudly displaying in sunlight the name LUSITANIA in curving gold lettering. The four funnels let out thick smoke that swept around four dragon-like clouds in the blue sky, and seemed to say 'Beware!' The liner emitted many blasts of its whistle as the flags high on their mastheads fluttered in the gentle breeze.

After a short time, the liner was rumbling loudly and the pier disappearing into the distance with the other vessels tied up in the docks. I felt a bit sad leaving New York and wondered when I would see it again. But the oral message from the engine room had to be delivered, which I did pronto, and then stood outside the wheel-room awaiting further orders.

As the liner's course proceeded smoothly over the water, passengers walked along the decks, heading for lunch, which was being announced by the galley stewards. Children played games in the enclosed decks, supervised by other stewards. As the *Lusitania* passed the Statue of Liberty, I stared at the lady in flowing robes with the crown of spikes on her head, holding up a torch with her bare right arm, and I whispered my farewell to Lady Liberty and New York.

CHAPTER 19

PENNY AND FINNY

I loved my work, bringing messages in yellow envelopes to and fro between the bridge and the Marconi Room and delivering service orders from the bars and restaurants for passengers in their cabins. The good thing about that was the tips. I quickly learnt from the other bellboys to be first, fast and friendly. That was our motto. We laughed, saying, 'FFF' as we passed each other in the corridors.

There was a lot of work, but it was also good fun, and my energy was boundless for running up and down flights of steps to the upper and lower decks. The deck floors had narrow strips of pale wood that looked beautiful. I passed lifeboat bays, each with a boat on hoists, with chains and ropes that swung slightly and rattled noisily, but not as loudly as the liner itself.

These lifeboats often set me brooding, but keeping busy made me forget about them. My journeys took me to every part of the ship and would have been a total joy but for the gnawing feeling, deep down, that something was not right. There were large deck lights showing up parts of the vessel, especially the funnels that seemed to touch the dark clouds high in the sky before dusk. When I came to the deck rail, there in front of me was the vast expanse of sea, with its billowing waves, and below me the steady throbbing of the liner and the hiss of the seawater. The sea air was almost overwhelming because it was so fresh – it seemed to almost suck my life out.

In the Verandah Café, on the first night, the orchestra struck up a lively melody entitled 'The Lusitania Two Step', and there were couples dancing. It was almost seven o'clock and I was still in uniform as I ran towards the games room so as not to be late meeting Penny Mayberry. She was on her way too, and we met by chance in front of a poster announcing a 'Sunday Afternoon Concert'. Her blue blazer had a crest with an eagle on the pocket that I hadn't noticed on our first meeting. She told me it was her school uniform and asked me where I went to school. I said that I went to Queenstown school. She asked me if it was a good school, and I said yes, and that Chalky Dempsey was very strict. I didn't mention her brother John in case she might go and fetch him. We walked over and back on the promenade deck because Penny was cold. I turned down two FFFs for passengers, saying that I was off duty. It was my first time ever alone with a girl and I really liked being with her.

In one of the cafés, as night descended, we ordered ice-cream sodas and toffee cake. I paid the bill and felt like my father, flashing my money around – nearly everything I had made on tips during the afternoon. But I didn't care. We sat at a round table amidst the crowds in an enclosed deck that was a lot cosier than walking in the cold. It had grown very chilly outside and a gale had begun to blow up.

'Let's face it, Finny, this situation is critical,' Penny stated. She called me 'Finny' because she said the name 'Finbar' sounded like a place that sold beer. Penny was very bossy at times, I discovered, and that made me want to be bossy too. 'Critical' was a word she used a lot. 'Something critical is going on that I want to tell you about. Mom has a second sense about these things. You can't visit with me and my Mom. She's minding John and stays in her cabin. Mom is not very well and that's why we're going to England – to stay with her sister there for a few months so that she can have a lot of rest – and recover.' I could see that she really needed to talk to someone and that she relaxed in my company.

'C-C-Critical about what?' I asked, trying to say the word correctly. I stared into Penny's eyes, and that made me forget what I wanted to say next.

'Okay, Finny, I will tell you.' She flicked her hair away from her face, and leaned forward, pushing away the soda glasses. 'Mom read the critical notice in the *New York Times*, the warning from the Germans about attacking liners that fly the British flag, and Mom feels that something will happen. She thinks we should have got off in New York, but Dad persuaded her that it would all be okay, that the notice was just cheap propaganda.' She stared at me intently. 'But I know something is going to happen.'

I gasped because Penny was expressing my own deepest fears.

'Look, Finny,' she continued, 'I've met senators, politicians, FBI people and all sorts of big people. I know about stuff through my folks. I think the *Lusitania* is carrying millions of dollars worth of gold in the cargo and arms for Britain. I'm sure of it, but you must help me find it and be absolutely certain. You can go into the cargo area and I can't.' I stared at her. 'It's difficult not to hear secret stuff when your dad is a senator. And Mom knows Pierpoint, the liner's detective; she calls him a pipe-smoking cop.' Penny laughed and then became serious. 'Mom thinks Aleister Crowley is a buffoon, but that notice of his scared her.'

I could have listened to her voice all night she was so amazing and suddenly she touched me on the knuckles and I put out my hand and touched hers.

'What are you doing,' she said, pulling back from me. 'Have you got a little princess in Queenstown?' She laughed and I felt my face going pale, and she began to look the same way. 'Let's go somewhere on our own,' she said. 'Let's go to the games room since there will be no kiddies there at this time of night.'

She got up and I walked beside her. She was silent the whole time and when I glanced at her, she looked crossly at me, but also laughed wildly. The games room was shut but there was a porch leading into it where there were two slatted benches. We sat down near a huge pane of glass that looked out on the dark night-time sea, with a view of waves because the lights of the liner lit up some of the seascape nearby. I told her everything about my time in New York, what I knew about the Baroness and the German codebook, about Crowley's gun cane, and my dreams of the shipwreck. I talked and talked, and when I had finished she looked at me solemnly.

'We were so stupid to get on this ship,' she said sadly, in

a way that scared me. 'We should have stayed at home.' Her face was so white it shone. I placed a hand on her cheek and she smiled as we held hands for a special moment. Then we walked along the decks towards her cabin.

'My dad knows how the world works, Finny. He is a senator, as I've told you. He knows President Woodrow Wilson,' she said, explaining that Wilson was the American president. 'My dad feels we are safe because the British Navy will protect the *Lusitania* because there are Americans on board, and maybe he's right, especially if there's gold bullion and arms on board too for the war.' She went silent then, and I wished that she would talk all night. 'We must find out, Finny.'

'How old are you?' she asked suddenly. 'I will be fifteen in June,' she said, running her fingers through her hair.

'I-I-I am fourteen,' I lied, feeling young and stupid all of a sudden.

'Right,' she said, 'you look fifteen, actually. How come you were a stowaway if your father is the Staff Captain?' She grinned at me.

'Well, I ran away from home after my father, but he didn't know until I was found in the cargo deck on the liner. The police in Ireland were searching for me. I left a note under my pillow at home ...' I didn't finish my story.

'Really,' she chuckled. 'You are an adventurer, aren't you Finny!' Then she told me about getting time off school while they were in England.

'Finny!' she whispered, 'we must be very careful. We sort of know a lot of dangerous stuff about spies, codebooks, weapons, gold and the war. And you're going to check it all out.' Suddenly she began to sound anxious. She said she had to go check up on her Mom and her tone of voice told me that I should not walk her to their cabin door.

That night I stole down to the cargo hold. The crewman on duty was kept busy helping himself to the sandwiches I had brought him. I told him I had been sent down to get something. I crept quietly along the passageway behind him to the point where Dad had stopped me, and there I saw packing cases marked *Remington Rifle Cartridges 1000*. Others were marked *Shrapnel Cases 500, Explosive Fuses 750*. These were arms! Then I counted six crates of gold bullion, each marked *Fort Knox* and *$1 Million in Gold Bar*. This was amazing. Penny was right.

I stayed awake until Dad arrived in our cabin for bed. 'Dad,' I said, 'I saw the ammunition and gold in the cargo room.

What is it for? I'm scared, Dad.'

'Okay, Finbar, that's dangerous information and I'd prefer if you didn't know it. You must realise how important it is. You must tell nobody. I am sure I can trust you totally. It's all very simple.' Dad looked sharply at me. 'The gold is for the Bank of England from the Bank of America and the US Treasury. War funding,' he said quietly, leaning across to me. 'War costs a lot of money and this is American help with the war effort.'

I blinked. This was crazy. What was I caught up in? What was my dad caught up in?

CHAPTER 20

SPIES AND LIES

I returned from a service cabin call to the first class saloon with a tray of plates, glasses and cutlery. The saloon was crowded with passengers dining and the orchestra was playing music in the background. I was told to polish glasses that had been drying until they shone. When this was done, I could knock off duty.

Suddenly, two of the liner's officers, Bestic and Lewis, along with Dad and Mr Pierpoint, marched through the crowded saloon, zigzagging around tables where people were chatting and enjoying their food. Dad went over to the man playing the piano, who held up a hand, and the orchestra stopped playing. Then my father, with Bestic and Lewis by his side, called out the names of two passengers – Mr Stahl and Mr Koenig –

who sat at a table with their drinks. Stahl was smoking. The two men stood up in alarm when Pierpoint held up a gun. Then, to my great surprise, my father pushed one of them to the ground and pointed a gun at his head. Everyone went silent and began to gape.

Pierpoint and my father leant against a table to steady themselves against the motion of the ship as they pointed their weapons. A jug of water fell over and I heard the trickle of the water because everything was so quiet, except for the ship's engines humming. Bestic produced two sets of handcuffs and snapped them on Stahl and Koenig. Dad held the gun menacingly in front of the two handcuffed men as Captain Turner and some other crew rushed in. The men were led out in handcuffs by Bestic and Lewis while Pierpoint walked behind them, holding his gun. It was quite a scary sight.

As soon as the door closed, the saloon came alive with gossip as to what the men in handcuffs might have done, and the word 'German spies' was on everyone's lips. Captain Turner went up to the bandstand and put his hand up for silence. 'Ladies and Gentlemen, please do not be alarmed. We have arrested two suspects, as you have witnessed. I am sorry we had to do this in front of you. For your safety these persons will spend the remainder of the voyage in the cells, under lock and key, and they will be handed over to MI5 in Liverpool. Anyone who would like a drink at the bar, please come and get one with our compliments. I am declaring a happy hour. Now let the music continue.' He smiled and everyone clapped with relief as the orchestra started to play again.

Dad came over to me and told me to report to the wheel-room as soon as I was off duty in the saloon. So I rushed there later and Dad, Captain Turner and Mr Pierpoint were sitting in the map room across from the liner's operations centre. I never got access to the operations centre because in there the elite crew steered the *Lusitania* across the Atlantic. The map room was a calmer place and the green baize table was lit from above by a gas lamp.

'Crew, our task is to get the *Lusitania* across the Atlantic safely.' Captain Turner plopped three lumps of sugar into the cup of tea I had brought him, and sipped from it. 'We must all be on extra alert. Every crew member has an important part to play in maintaining our safety. Finbar, may I remind you to make sure that all telegrams other than *Lusitania* business have been read by Mr Pierpoint. Okay? Show everything to Mr Pierpoint before you deliver it to McCormick.'

'Yes, Captain,' I said, feeling that I had a very important role to play.

CHAPTER 21

PENNY'S WARNING

After my work was over I went to the Mayberrys' cabin and knocked. There was no reply for ages. Then Penny, looking sleepy and dressed in her pyjamas and dressing gown, opened the door.

'I can't talk, Finny,' she said in a loud whisper. 'You need to go away. Mom is worried to distraction...' I heard Mrs Mayberry's voice calling her. 'No! Wait here a few minutes,' she said, shutting the door. I walked up and down the corridor, ready to run if any other door opened, in case I might be seen loitering about while off duty and get reported. At last, Penny opened the door. 'Come in quickly,' she whispered. 'I told Mom a little white lie that I have ordered hot chocolate to help me sleep.'

'I can go and get you hot chocolate,' I insisted, but she put a hand to my mouth to stop me talking, and said: 'No! Ssshh!'

'In here, Finny.' She beckoned me forward. I crept quietly into her room where her bed was neatly made up and the book *Little Women* lay on the pillows. There were two chairs, on one of which was a bulky suitcase. The curtains were drawn across the window and the liner made great thudding noises while the ocean boomed and hissed outside. She put the suitcase in a closet, moved the chairs side by side and we sat down. I think she moved the chairs together so we didn't need to talk out loud which might have woken her mother and John.

'If Mom calls, you can hide. She is so tired she won't notice anything. What did you find out, Finny?' She looked at me and her neatly combed hair seemed longer over her dressing gown that had the same crest as her school blazer, of the eagle in pine-trees. When I looked at her feet she pushed them into fluffy slippers. I stared at her eyes, forgetting her question for a moment, but it soon came back to my mind.

'There *are* guns and ammunition and gold on board,' I said. 'I saw them in cargo. Dad told me not to tell anyone.' I felt bad betraying him, but I just had to tell Penny. 'I am having bad dreams,' I went on. 'One about a submarine below in the ocean. I saw it fire arrows at a liner.'

'Was it *our* liner in your dream?' Her eyes seemed to glow with specks of fire as she asked me. 'Was there a shipwreck?'

'I don't think it was our liner. Maybe it was, I don't know,' I also remembered dreaming about *her*, but did not mention this.

'Mom thinks it is all very critical. She is fearful …' she moved closer so that her face was at my shoulder and I could feel the scent of her breath that reminded me of apples. 'Mom thinks that the Germans might attack us.'

Too much was going on for me all of a sudden: German spies, British spies, the codebook, the weapons and ammunition and American gold for England's war.

'Listen, Finny, it's getting a bit complicated,' Penny said seriously. 'Mom says that there's a conspiracy, and that people are saying that we Americans are a target not only for the Germans but for the British too! If this liner is attacked it will be seen as an attack on America. And that means America will enter the war. So each side wants the *Lusitania* attacked!' She paused to let me catch up.

'But why? And how?' I must have seemed very stupid, but she simply smiled, held my hand, and then for a moment put her head on my shoulder while she gave a little yawn.

'Look, the *Lusitania* is full of VIP Americans and British

– we are the cheese, Mom says, for the big mouse: either Germany or Britain. Germany wants to attack us because America supports Britain in the war, even though we're not actually fighting in it. Britain might want us attacked to force us into the war. That's what Mom said anyway. I don't know if she's gone a bit crazy, Finny.' She sat straight in her chair once more and smoothed her dressing gown.

'Britain would never let the Germans blow up one of her own liners – that's mad! And the British Navy will be there to protect us. That's what Dad told me,' I said forcefully. 'And what about the passengers and the crew? What about you and me, Penny?' I was afraid of what I was thinking all of a sudden.

She looked intently at me, her eyes seeming to be fixed on something in the distance, and then, as if she was sleepwalking, her lips moved towards mine and she kissed me. My whole body shivered. She withdrew then and we both smiled. I longed to kiss her again like that, but she stood up, with a finger to her lips.

We left her room and walked up and down in the corridor for a while, holding hands. The only sounds were of the *Lusitania* plunging through the ocean. Finally she stopped in front of her cabin.

I couldn't think of anything to say, but I wanted to say

something before she went in.

'Thanks for telling me so much, Penny. You know more than the *New York Times*.'

She laughed. 'Good night, Finny.' She gave a slight nod of her head and shut the door behind her, locking it with a click from inside. I waited and listened, and wanted to knock and go back in, but withdrew and ran to my bunk for a night's rest before work in the morning.

That night the liner rolled and pitched quite a bit, snagging back with a shudder sometimes that made it hard for me to get any sleep. Dad was on night watch in the wheel-room. I sat up in my bunk and stared out the porthole window, drawing back the curtain noisily on its rail. The glass was speckled in water drops and beyond it the menacing sea swirled crazily. I longed to be home in Queenstown, but felt it was so far away. Even after reaching Liverpool, Dad and I would have to catch another boat home to Queenstown. It seemed such a long journey. Five hundred miles and more, I'd heard in the captain's den. Hurry on, liner, and keep us safe, I prayed. I had heard too much and understood too much now because of Penny. I just wanted the journey to be over.

CHAPTER 22

THE TIN FISH

The German naval Kapitän, Walther Schwieger, was in the depths of the ocean in the German submarine, U-boat 20, buttoning his black tunic against the cold. He was a thin-lipped, small man, with fair hair and a deep scar across one cheek, slanting from the left eye to under his ear; the scar came from a knife fight he'd had with another sailor when he was young. He patted his dog, Hooper, a white *dachshund,* and fondled the animal's soft ears. There were four officers and thirty-one men on board the U-20, as well as the dog. Schwieger had smuggled Hooper onto the submarine – it was against German naval regulations to have a dog on board but Schwieger thought that Hooper would be good for morale. He glanced at a magazine press-cutting wrapped in grimy cellophane on a shelf. In the photograph was Monika von Leiditz in her wedding dress standing beside her eldest sister, Baroness Leonie von Leiditz. Schwieger stood proudly, his arm linked with Monika's, glancing at her with a smile. The marriage had been a news item in the society pages of the press, and Schwieger was proud of it.

The crew were careful how they treated Hooper as they feared Schwieger's continuous outburts of anger since leaving the German naval base of Wilhelmshaven. Their mission was to destroy British battleships, and orders from Berlin arrived in code. The book used to decode the messages was in a steel container the size of a lunch box.

The U-20 was on a course on the Irish Sea, passing the coast of County Wexford and heading south. Rations were low, and, besides, it was poor food. The fresh-water supply was also dwindling. When the cold, dry sausages and biscuits were passed out amongst the crew, even Hooper did not beg and pant as usual, but sniffed the air and looked around.

Life on board was cramped. The walls of the submarine were awash with condensation. It was like being in a damp cellar day after day and never being able to get any fresh air. When the sailors were off duty, they lay in their bunks almost as lifeless as the torpedoes which were stacked in steel racks like huge shelves, just off the gangway of the U-boat. Sometimes they woke up coughing up mucus as if they had a heavy cold, and they had to drink castor oil to keep their stomachs from erupting.

Secrecy, silence, especially radio silence had to be kept, sometimes for hours in case British battleships and U-boat destroyers on the surface discovered the presence of the U-boat below. This could easily happen when the U-boat was at periscope depth, only twelve feet down, which was the depth they had to stay at, waiting and watching for ships in order to sink them.

'Kapitän Schwieger,' called out the radio operator suddenly. 'I have a message for decoding.' Schwieger passed him the key to the steel box which the operator opened; then he took out the codebook and began 'translating' into readable words: 'Lusitania in your zone from 7 May. Take up position to sink Lusitania. Return to base if you fail. By orders of Admiral von Tirpitz.'

'When did you get this?' Schwieger yelled at the man.

'Just now, Kapitän,' the operator stuttered. 'I can seek further orders if you wish, sir.'

'I will give the orders now. The Lusitania is the fastest liner on the high seas. It can go three times as fast as we can. But we will go after it. We will fulfil the order from high command.'

'But, Kapitän Schwieger, it is a passenger liner!'

'Any British ship that enters the war zone is the enemy. We must destroy every enemy of Germany if the German people are to avenge the wrongs done to us by our enemies. Do we all understand?'

'Yes, Kapitän,' shouted the crew.

'We will keep awake. We will keep watch for days. Our stomachs may creak with hunger, but we will wait. We will sink the *Lusitania* as instructed. And I will get my iron cross for doing my duty for Germany and for the Kaiser.'

CHAPTER 23

WAITING FOR THE ROYAL NAVY

'Finbar, Finbar.' I felt someone tugging at my sleeve. It was my father and he looked anxious. 'You were talking in your sleep, Finbar. Are you all right? I have to go to the wheel-room. Dawn is breaking so you need to get up. Today we enter the war zone. You will be expected to keep watch with the rest of the crew, as well as do your other duties.'

'I had an awful dream,' I told him.

'Many of us are having dreams about submarines, Finbar. Don't worry about it. I have to go. Make sure you report to the chief steward as soon as you're ready.' Dad brushed his jacket, straightened his peaked cap and went out. The cabin door slammed with the jolting of the liner and the noise brought me to my senses. Dreams, visions – whatever – I had better get to work. I washed, as usual, with the basin half-full of water as Dad had shown me in case it spilled with the movement of the liner. My tunic needed a good brushing, as did my trousers, and I had to polish my boots. Then I proudly donned my cap, straightened my collar, and combed my hair. I was ready for work.

I walked out on the top deck past some passengers who were still in evening clothes. They must have been up very late at one of the parties in the Verandah Café or in the first class lounge. These were two places that the other bellboys and I vied for as the tips were always generous, especially from Americans and the Hollywood movie people who gave us more than the usual dollar or 50 cents, especially as the night wore on.

I paused, looking out at the vast expanse of sea. It was the seventh day of our voyage from New York. I had got used to the daily aspect of seascape and was reassured by the mighty liner ploughing onwards, ever onwards. I saw some passengers standing at the railings and pointing, and sure enough there was the far off sight of land! What a rare sight. I was very excited after so many days surrounded by nothing but sea and sky. Then came a swirl of gulls, far out from what must be Ireland's shores. They swerved and swayed above the four stacks to avoid the guttering smoke that came from the chimneys. The top deck glistened in morning light. I passed the lifeboats that hung like huge white baskets covered in oval canvas hoods. Ireland and home were not too far away.

A steward was in the crew's galley eating a fried egg, bacon and beans on toast. He sipped a mug of tea and gave me orders to take Captain Turner his breakfast. While I waited for the food to be cooked and laid out on a tray, one of the cooks gave me a bacon sandwich with a thick slice of cheese and a glass of milk that I gorged down quickly, wiping my mouth after it. I arranged the tray for Captain Turner with his porridge, grilled kippers, brown toast with butter and marmalade, pot of tea and jug of milk.

'Ah Finbar, well done,' said Captain Turner when I arrived with the tray. He was reading a weather chart on his desk. 'Is my tea strong enough so that you could trot a mouse on it?'

'Aye, aye, Captain!' I replied, leaving the tray beside his binoculars, his twenty-four hour clock, papers, documents, and a navigational map of the Atlantic, Ireland and Britain. The *Lusitania Log Book*, a black-covered ledger, was open and Captain Turner asked me to fetch a pen and ink from a shelf.

I waited to run other errands as he ate the porridge. Then he picked at the kippers with the fork and bit into some toast, leaving the crusts, before writing in the liner's log. On a new page he wrote: 7 May 1915. Time: 07.24. His handwriting was very neat:

> *So far so good, entering Irish waters. Crew excellent, morale high. Passengers slightly anxious. Occasional complaints and worries about the possibilities of attack from U-boats. My plans are to maintain a steady course and keep close to top speed around the south coast of Ireland and we have reserves of fuel for final docking in Liverpool tomorrow, God willing.*

'Take this chart up to the wheel-room.' The captain suddenly snapped out an order, then, in a more kindly voice, added, 'Leave the tray, Finbar.' I clambered up two flights of iron stairs and into the wheel-room, panting. My father was there and he unrolled the chart, then went over to talk to Officer Bestic, who was steering a coarse due south of Valentia, the first lighthouse in Irish waters. I heard them discussing the details. My joy increased as I knew we were nearing home, but fear also gripped me.

'How are the sea conditions, Jack?' Captain Turner burst in the door. Dad muttered positively and alongside him Bestic held the wheel. All three men stared ahead and the great liner trundled along, unstoppable, it seemed to me, so I felt all might be well.

'She is at a goodly cruising speed of twenty-one knots, three knots short of maximum capacity,' I heard Bestic shout out in a joyous mood.

'We can expect to see Valentia Lighthouse within the hour. We'll be glad to be on the final leg of the journey,' my father muttered to Turner, who nodded vigorously.

'Amen to that,' the Captain said as McCormick rushed in from the Marconi room with a sheet of paper in his hand.

'You must read this message, Captain, sir.' McCormick was flustered and his voice quivered.

'Show me.' Captain Turner grabbed the bulletin page that had been signed by the radio operator and exhaled heavily.

'What does it say?' my father asked, frowning.

'It's from Valentia: *Submarines active off south coast of Ireland.*' Captain Turner's voice was sharp. 'Hold the present course. Keep our speed up. I'll call all the officers to the bridge. We'll need to order some more of the crew on deck-watch duty.' The Captain lifted the binoculars to his eyes and scanned the sea ahead. 'At least the sea's fairly calm. Visibility is good. I need another weather report. And, McCormick, cable Valentia for every sighting of submarines they possess. Hurry, man!'

McCormick nearly knocked me over as he ran out, and no sooner had the door of the wheel-room slammed behind him than it opened again and in filed all the liner's officers for emergency duty. Turner gave each an order, and each one nodded silently and quickly went out to organise the crewmen for the deck watch.

'We will have naval support soon.' Captain Turner picked up his binoculars after some minutes of silence in the wheel-room. I felt weak with fear. I had been given no orders yet, so I waited. Should I say something about my dreams? About Penny's fears? About her mother's crazy ideas? I wished I could speak to Penny because she'd know what to do. The liner sailed on and a haze developed which soon became a thick, foggy swirl, with the sun's disc becoming a silver pennant in the morning behind the vast curtain of fog. Suddenly the horizon narrowed and long-range visibility was gone. The curtain of smoky fog became our only sight. Bestic repeatedly rang the foghorn. It was a gloomy, droning sound, a groan above the liner's churning noise.

'Another message!' McCormick burst into the wheel-room and everyone moved out of his way.

'What?' gasped Captain Turner when he read the message. '*Reduce speed.* But why?' He read the message again and looked aghast at my father. 'This is an order from British Naval Intelligence that we must slow our speed. Why? But I have to obey orders, damn it!' The Captain shouted out a message on the tannoy that would transmit his orders to the engine room.

'Perhaps it will help the naval escort to find us more easily?' my father suggested, but his voice had a worried tone.

'It seems a dangerous course to follow,' Captain Turner answered. 'I shall stay close by the Irish coastline as we have been ordered for the morning. Where is the convoy of battleships to protect us?' He banged the desk with his fist.

Yes, I thought, good question, where were the British battleships? I ran messages all morning from the wheel-room to the Marconi room, but there were no further important messages.

Around noon the Captain called all the officers to the wheel-room again. He checked through everything with them in turn: 'The deck watch is in place? The passengers are calm and comfortable? The orchestra is playing? The children are at their games and recreation?' Yes, Captain, came the answers. 'Tell the galley not to spare anything,' he continued. 'Let the food be the best the dining rooms and buffets can offer.' Captain Turner's voice changed suddenly as he took a deep breath: 'It is alarming that the Royal Navy has sent no battleships or submarine destroyers to protect us yet. And I do not understand this order to reduce our speed. However, we will keep our nerve and get the liner into land. I have alerted the engine room to slow down. We have reserve steam and if we see a German U-boat, we can muster almost twice their speed if we have to make a dash for Queenstown in case Liverpool is too risky a venture, being the furthest port of call. Get out the relevant maps, please. Now, return to your posts and keep up the deck watch. Anything that looks even vaguely like a periscope on top of the ocean, send your fastest runner to tell Captain Kennedy and me, understood?'

'Finbar,' he gestured towards me, 'run to McCormick. Ask him about further sightings of German submarines. Stay there until he has up-to-date news on this situation. Understood?'

'Yes sir, Captain Turner,' I said, and raced off to do his bidding.

I reached the Marconi room and noticed the clock: 12.11. McCormick was ready with a pencil between his fingers for any message that might come. Suddenly the machine began to vibrate and tap. McCormick carefully wrote down each word. I did not dare open my mouth.

'Rush this message to Captain Turner!' he screamed. I took the paper, folded it quickly and pushed it deep in my pocket. This time I ran so fast I nearly fell on the steps up to the wheel-room but caught myself, tugged out the message and rushed in. I handed it over. Turner read it out loud and his voice became shrill: '*Submarines active in the Irish Channel, twenty miles south of Coningbeg Lightship*. That's where we're passing now,' Captain Turner's voice was tense. My father and Turner stared at the fog bank. The horizon was still lost and merged with the sky as in the landscape of a dream. Captain Turner pressed the binoculars to his eyes. 'Where are we?' he asked Dad, who was studying a chart carefully. 'Why is there no further message from Naval Intelligence and why is there is no sign of the British Navy?' Turner shouted, hitting his forehead with the palm of one hand.

'I think we must be near Kinsale,' said Dad. 'At least, my reckoning tells me so.' He wrote calculations with a pencil as he moved a ruler and dividers rapidly across the chart.

'Right, Jack,' said Turner. 'Look,' he suddenly shouted, so loudly his voice became hoarse, and pointed to the landmass barely visible far off across the waves. 'It's the Old Head of Kinsale. It must be! Am I glad to see the lighthouse!'

'You're right. It would be impossible to mistake the Old

Head of Kinsale even in this fog,' said Dad to the Captain, and both men sounded relieved.

'I reckon,' Turner said with resolution, 'we should set a straight course for half an hour. Pray to God that we sight a Royal Navy battleship soon.' Captain Turner and my father both looked through their binoculars while Officer Bestic steered, gripping the wheel firmly. I bit my lip and felt queasy. I could hardly get off duty at such a critical time to go and look for Penny, but I wished that I could.

CHAPTER 24

ATTACK!

K apitän Schwieger stood in the periscope bay. His hands were on the handles of the periscope, the U-boat's visual link to the top of the sea.

'Klaus,' he called to one of the officers, 'quick, take a look!' The U-20 approached a position ten miles off the Old Head of Kinsale. There was the *Lusitania*.

'Yes, Kapitän, she is a beauty,' Klaus shrieked, 'but she is turning away from us.' Klaus moved away from the periscope to let the Kapitän see for himself.

'Increase our sped to twelve knots!' screamed Schwieger.

Klaus spun a wheel and drew down a switch. He pulled back another lever and looked at dials as the speed increased from the four diesel engines. The U-boat throbbed, hummed and vibrated. Hooper, the *dachshund*, aroused himself and looked about.

'*Mein Gott!*' said Schwieger as he watched the huge hull and bulk of the liner enter his sights in the lens of the periscope. 'Battle stations! *Achtung!*' he shouted. 'Prepare to load the torpedo shafts. Everything is going according to plan.'

Four men lifted torpedoes to the round hatches and pushed in the sleek, conical-headed cylinders, marked with the word *trotyl* and, in large letters, T. N. T. printed beside a red skull logo.

'Torpedoes loaded, Kapitän,' shouted Klaus, wiping his sweating face with an oily rag.

'Turn rudder five degrees to port. *Schnell! Schnell,*' shrieked Schwieger as Hooper pricked up his ears. 'Steady rudder, steady speed. *Achtung.* Attack the *Lusitania*! Prepare to fire torpedoes. Fire one!'

All eyes watched. Hooper stood up, his tail wagging. The torpedo shot out of the firing tube and entered the ocean, making the submarine shudder. The torpedo hit the underwater surge of pressure with a hiss, sending a trail of bubbles past the portholes.

'We will have to wait a few seconds and see how good our aim is,' Schwieger's voice screamed.

'Kapitän, it cannot miss. Look closely,' Klaus's confidence of a hit was infectious.

'And if this torpedo misses we can fire another – and another. I will have my iron cross,' Schweiger bellowed and turned to Klaus. He reached for the photograph of Monika, the Baroness, Klaus and himself. He kissed it, pushed it into his tunic pocket and stared through the periscope with intense excitement.

DISASTER!

CHAPTER 25

SOS LUSITANIA

'Torpedo coming on the starboard side!' Two crewmen on the deck below me shouted up and I ran for the stairs to tell Captain Turner. The news was screamed from one voice to another so that by the time I reached the wheel-room the Captain already knew. The liner suddenly jolted and shuddered, then shook with a deep groan. It strained to keep its speed, then lurched to one side as a terrific explosion rang out. A huge crack appeared in the top deck. Debris and water shot up, hit the mast and drenched the flags, turning them into coloured bits of rag. I thought of the warning in the newspapers.

'Turn about and make a dash for harbour,' Captain Turner shouted to Officer Bestic. 'We have been hit by a torpedo! We are only TEN miles off Kinsale. Hard-a-starboard!' He kept repeating this. 'Finbar,' he ordered, 'run to the Marconi room and tell McCormick to send an SOS to Kinsale. Keep sending it: *SOS Lusitania, emergency*.' Captain Turner stared at me, and there was no mistaking the shock in his eyes.

This time I fell on my way because of the crowds out on deck, all with anxious faces and asking questions of the stewards and the crew. I picked myself up quickly from the deck. My uniform hat was on the deck and I shoved it back on. McCormick was at the door of the Marconi room, heard my message and rushed inside. I shouted to him to keep transmitting the SOS signal.

When I reached the wheel-room again, Captain Turner and Officer Bestic were both pulling at the wheel, their faces damp with perspiration. 'The wheel is jammed. The torpedo damaged the controls. We cannot steer!' Captain Turner shouted at Dad, who rushed over and put his hands to the wheel too, but it was useless. 'Steam pressure has dropped by sixty percent. We're losing all power,' shouted Captain Turner to my father, who just shook his head, unable to answer. I did not believe what was happening – my dreams and the warning notice were all coming true!

Suddenly there was a huge explosion down in the engine

rooms and the liner lost all speed, drifted and tilted over. I turned and looked out of the window and saw fire shoot out from the chimneystacks. The mighty *Lusitania* slumped over on her starboard side. I looked back towards the Captain and my father, hoping desperately that they would have some plan of action.

'I'm giving the order to abandon ship,' shouted Captain Turner. 'I don't know how long she can stay afloat.'

My father took me by the arm and dragged me outside. 'Finbar, you go to the boat deck. Get a lifebelt on you. Join a queue with the bellboys. Go now, hurry. I will get to safety later...' his voice failed him.

'Dad, what will happen to us? I want to stay with you.' I stared into his face, feeling more frightened than ever before in my life.

'Finbar, go now. Do what I say. I must do my duty as Staff Captain. Go!' He ran off. I stood looking after him as he disappeared along the deck among the crowd. His disappearance spurred me into action. I remembered two things: first, there were lifebelts in our cabin, and second I wanted to get the toys we had got for Colleen, Christopher and Sean – the accordion, cowboy outfit and rocking horse! But the toys were in the cargo deck and I realised that I'd have to forget about them. Most importantly, I desperately wanted to go to Penny's cabin and check on her. How could I do that?

The liner tilted further with a lurch, but I could still get to our cabin under the boat deck. The cabin door had burst open and the bunks had fallen on the floor, making it easier to pull out the lifebelts from underneath. Awkwardly I put the lifebelt on – little had I thought that I would ever wear one for real!

CHAPTER 26

LIFEBOATS

I scrambled up to the boat deck as a steward was shouting out orders to crewmen. 'There are over two thousand passengers in first, second and third class, as well as forty-five children and forty infants. There are seven hundred crew. We need to mingle among the passengers and keep the queues orderly. Hey you,' he shouted at me, 'you are crew. Wait until all passengers are safely in the lifeboats. You must not get aboard a lifeboat until instructed. You have not been trained how to command a lifeboat.' I moved away from the crowds of passengers and tried to cling on to hope. The Irish coast seemed very far away, but luckily the fog had lifted.

Crewmen rushed about and passengers clung onto handrails or made their way with difficulty along where chairs and tables were gathered in broken heaps against the railings because the liner was tilting so far over towards the sea. Passengers looked pale with fear. The air was filled with screams and crying.

'Hurry! Put on your lifejackets,' shouted the crewmen repeatedly. The last piles of lifejackets were grabbed by people at the end of the queues. Each jacket was padded with cork, wrapped in tough canvas and had straps and a belt.

Suddenly, out of the darkness, explosions erupted in the boilers, and flames shot out of the chimneystacks like a fireworks display. Panic-stricken passengers stared in terror at the chimneys that seemed about to fall on top of them. I caught a glimpse of Captain Turner and my father shouting orders as they clung onto the railings outside the wheel-room.

Crewmen peeled off the huge canvas hoods from the last of the lifeboats and opened the deck railings which were the only barrier between the cold sea and us, hundreds of feet below. Women and children crowded into the boats and sat along the benchlike seats. 'Each boat can only take seventy,' I heard a crewman say, counting people as they passed him. When a lifeboat was filled with women and children, the ropes and pulleys lowered the boat until it landed safely in the water.

Within the chaos of the liner, the crew kept pushing people into the remaining lifeboats and screaming, 'Lower away, lower away for Chrissake.' As before, the boats moved down towards the water on creaking ropes with jerks and jolts. In one of the lifeboats that was already in the sea, Evangelical women led the survivors in a chorus of the hymn: 'There is a Green Hill Far Away'. Kinsale was ten miles away, and that was a long distance to row with seventy people in a boat. The land seemed very far away indeed and I wondered would I ever reach it?

CHAPTER 27

THE SEAL MAN

By now I was feeling desperate. I was on my own, without my father or my friend Penny or even another crew member. As the very last lifeboat was being loaded I watched it fill up, but crew members were not allowed on board, there were too many passengers. Where were the rest of the lifeboats? I wondered. Probably buried under the ship.

When the number on the lifeboat had reached seventy-three, including men, women and children, the overcrowded boat was lowered. The deck sloped at such an angle that I felt weak in the stomach. The people aboard clung to one another until they reached the surface of the sea. I knew then that it would be sink or swim for me, and for all of us left without a lifeboat to board. I wasn't a great swimmer, but I had no choice but to try.

Then the strangest thing happened. From a stairhead that was tilted because the liner slumped forward, came a man dressed like a seal, dragging a huge trunk along. As he got closer to me I could see that he had a thick suit of black rubber covering him from head to foot, with openings for his eyes, mouth and nose. He wore a pair of goggles. He opened the trunk and with great exertion heaved out a bulky coil of brown rubber that had loops of rope attached to it and two wooden paddles. Then he took out a small chest, like a treasure chest, edged with strips of metal. As those of us remaining on deck sought a place from which to jump into the sea, the Seal Man seemed to fidget and poke at the large coil of rubber. 'Here, hold this,' he ordered me, holding out a rope, and I gripped it as he thrust it into my hand. The lump of rubber soon puffed up into a small boat!

'Come with me, boy,' he said. 'Get in. You will be of help to me and you will not take up much weight.' From nowhere, it seemed, he pulled out a black net bag, stuffed the two paddles into it and slung it across his back.

'We will jump from here,' the seal man shouted when he found an empty lifeboat bay. 'I will push the boat over the side. As soon as you sight it in the water, jump in that direction. When you reach the water, swim for one of the loops of rope attached to the boat's sides and wait for me. Got it?' He spoke in military tones as if ordering soldiers, and I got the feeling he had done this before, he was so calm and cool. This was a great relief to me. I felt I could do this – it was my only chance of survival.

He pushed the boat over the side and it fluttered more than fell till it hit the water far below.

'Right,' he bellowed, checking quickly on the boat bobbing about on the ocean. 'Jump on the count of three – and jump far to the left and the boat will float back to us. Ready!' he shouted. 'One! Two! Three! Jump!'

On landing in the water I hit a broken deckchair floating there and felt a sharp pain in my ankle as I sank, then surfaced and bobbed up and down, gasping for air and spitting out a mouthful of seawater. I was not far from the rubber boat. I swam desperately towards it. The Seal Man was beside me in an instant.

'The boat landed upside down,' he shouted. 'We must turn it. I will submerge. Stay there.' He held his nose, flung himself forward and disappeared under the ocean soon to re-emerge with the net bag in his hand. He had taken it off his back. He pushed it into my hands.

'Now,' he said, 'pay attention.' Seawater and spittle lashed me from his mouth. 'I have to swim under the boat and flip it over. You, boy, must help me turn it. Hold that bag in one hand and push with the other. It might take a few attempts, but we must succeed. Go under the narrow end and raise the side of the boat as high as you can.' He dived under the boat and disappeared.

My ankle stung in pain but I had no choice but to follow orders. I pushed the side of the boat upwards as hard as I could, and somehow the boat, presumably because of the man's skill and practice, righted itself quickly, and was ready for boarding. The Seal Man pulled himself aboard along the narrow end of the boat and then he hauled me in. I was still clutching the bag with the paddles. He pulled the paddles out of the bag, pushed them through loops on either side of the boat and fastened them securely with ropes that passed through holes in the handles. Then he began to row furiously away from the sinking liner, past lifeboats and people clutching to lifebelts floating in the water. I was soaked to the skin and had a sore ankle, but I knew I was very lucky.

'Ten miles to row,' shouted the Seal Man. 'We'll make it safely to land, boy. It will take a few hours. Your job is to watch the coastline closely, boy, and keep track of where we're going. You'd better do it right or we're gone!'

Looking back at the *Lusitania* as he rowed us away I could see from our rubber boat that it was going to be a battle against the sea for each person stuck there, struggling in the water. My heart went out to them. Would any of them manage the long swim to shore? In the icy temperatures and with their soggy clothes and shivering bodies, I doubted it. Mothers with babies tried to hold them safely above the water line; the babies screamed in the cold and looked like plump, squealing fish. Some mothers had already drowned and their babies just floated away. I saw Nurse Ellis go underwater in the distance, and I gasped in shock. I ached to see Dad and Penny, but Nurse Ellis was the only person I recognised.

The Seal Man rowed on, and all the time we passed people who were panicking. They were spluttering and inhaling seawater through their mouths and noses, and I watched as some finally lost their breath in the panic. For minutes their arms slashed at the water and then stopped as they slumped over, face down in the sea, or else turned skywards, their heads thrown back, mouths open, with vacant, lifeless eyes. Gulls swooped towards some of the drowned who floated on the surface. I saw a gull shriek then perch on a man's shoulders near his upturned face. I looked away.

I stared and stared, transfixed, searching for my father as

some crewmen clung to the liner that began to shoot out flames. A boy stood on the burning deck and in a sudden movement fell from such a height I could not see where he hit the water. The chimneystacks loomed overhead from the tilting liner, and began to crack in two, falling headlong on top of people who screamed in terror. The wire cables that held the chimney stacks in position snapped as explosions rained on top of the remaining crew who were washed overboard into the waves from the doomed liner.

I turned around in the Seal Man's boat to watch more of the awful spectacle. Crewmen grabbed deckchairs and collapsible rafts while others fastened their lifejackets tightly, chose their spot in the water and jumped clear. I kept my eyes peeled for my father or Penny. The collapsible rafts were the only refuge for many, who swam towards them. Some people managed to grab onto them and held on for dear life. Others clutched desperately at anything that might keep them afloat and save them from a watery grave.

The liner, a vessel of such power and might, tilted so close to the sea's surface that she finally fell over into the water. This caused a mighty splash, as if a volcano was erupting from beneath the sea. A mound of foaming water sent swimmers, corpses, deckchairs and other wreckage churning to the surface as the sea level rose over the sinking wreck.

We rowed between the lifeboats and as we were much lower in the water we passed by unnoticed. We moved slowly away, and from under the water where the *Lusitania* had disappeared came a final loud explosion. My eyes filled up with tears. I was crying for my father and Penny – and for the horror that had unfolded in front of my eyes.

The Seal Man rowed like some inhuman creature in his suit of black skin, impervious to the cold. My ankle stung, but I didn't care. I began to wonder again who he was and how he had this life-saving equipment. Was he a spy? Had he been spying on board the *Lusitania*? I would probably never know. I was so exhausted from all the trauma that I felt myself sliding into a swoon of sleep and slumped over against the side of the boat.

I was awoken by a shout: 'Boy! Stay awake. Look for the shore at all times!'

CHAPTER 28

NEWS SPREAD FAR AND WIDE...

Sergeant Kilroy received news of the shipwreck from Admiral Coke's office in Queenstown as the cathedral bells chimed four o'clock.

...sunk by U-boat torpedo, off Kinsale Head. *Liner* disappeared under the water at 2.30pm. Hundreds of lives lost. Have dispatched vessels *Brock*, *Flying Fox* and *Golden Effort* to search for survivors. Alert hospitals and other shelters for survivors.

Signed: Admiral Sir Charles Coke, Queenstown, 7 May 1915

The sergeant rose in his chair and called a police officer to take over from him. Sergeant Kilroy took his bicycle and cycled along the quay, dismounting when he reached Hill Street. When he got to No. 1 Park Terrace, he left the bicycle by the side of the house and knocked. Mam opened the door, with Christopher by her side.

'I'd better come in, if I may?' The Sergeant took off his peaked cap gravely. 'Admiralty House received this message and sent us a copy. You'd better read it, Mrs Kennedy. How are you, Christopher?' He turned to the boy, but the little fellow ignored him and stared at his mother.

Mam read the message, looked at the Sergeant and put a hand to her forehead.

'Oh Mam!' shouted Colleen, arriving at the door, 'is it about Finbar? Is he all right?'

'No,' said Mam, walking slowly into the kitchen and sitting down at the table.

'No? Oh God, what's wrong with Finbar?' Colleen began to weep, and Mam did too, while Sean dropped his football and ran to his mother.

Mam held her children close to her, then composed herself and stopped crying, though there were still tears in her eyes. 'We know nothing yet, children. There has been a terrible tragedy at sea. The *Lusitania* has ...' She began to weep again.

'And Daddy ...?' Colleen looked at her mother who sobbed more loudly.

'You're a fine family,' said Sergeant Kilroy. He didn't know what else to say.

'When will Daddy and Finbar be home?' Christopher asked Sergeant Kilroy.

'Children, the *Lusitania* has sunk. That's all we know at this time. We must hope and pray that Daddy and Finbar have survived.'

'Admiral Coke's cable is all too true and all too shocking,' said the Sergeant. 'And it was only a few weeks ago we were all here looking for your Finbar ...' He picked up his peaked cap. 'Now we are searching for survivors. I suppose that is the way to look at it.'

Mam sighed and got up. 'Can I offer you a cup of tea, Sergeant?' She went towards the cooker for the kettle.

'No thanks, Mrs Kennedy,' he said. 'I have to go back to the barracks.' He put his cap on. Mam saw him to the door and spent a long time standing there, staring down at the harbour, until Colleen came out to her.

'Mam, what are we going to do?' she begged.

'I don't know, dear child. Will you run and get Mrs Kelly

and ask her to mind Sean? I want to go and look for our men,' she said mournfully. 'I need you with me, and Christopher. We'll go as soon as Mrs Kelly arrives. Hurry, Colleen.'

Mrs Kelly returned with Colleen, and she rushed in and hugged Mam. 'I heard the news about the awful tragedy, Kitty. The whole town is talking about it. You know nothing for certain yet, Kitty, so we'll all just keep hoping and praying.' Mrs Kelly's voice was low and her hair was tied up in a scarf. She had been baking and her hands were covered in dough. 'You go off with Christopher and Colleen, now. I'll bring Sean over to my house and he can help me a bit. I got a huge order from the hotels. Loads of tarts, I was just going to come for you, Kitty, to see if you'd help,' she explained. 'Would you like a currant bun, Sean?' Mrs Kelly put out her hand to Sean. 'Take a coat, Kitty, and warm clothes for the children.'

Outside the Kennedy house, the two women hugged each other.

'We'll hope for the best and prepare for the worst,' Mrs Kelly said, with sadness in her voice.

Mam, Colleen and Christopher walked quickly past the cathedral and took a short cut down a lane of steps onto Old

Street. They entered the Cunard offices on Westbourne Place where a queue was already forming. When the desk clerk listened to Mam and read her identity document bearing the name and rank of her husband, he came from behind the counter, pushed his way through the crowd and directed her to the park along the harbour edge. The Kennedys joined another crowd there, and an official from Cunard, in a uniform like a sea captain's, handed them three return tickets on the *Cork, Bandon and South Coast Railway* and omnibus services for Kinsale.

At the station, they waited with others for a special train that finally began shunting for Cork city after two hours. All the passengers spoke in low tones and many said nothing. In Cork it was raining and Mam was glad that she had the warm clothes. Colleen and her mother wrapped shawls about themselves while Christopher pulled on his flat cap. They climbed aboard the omnibus beneath the signboard marked Kinsale. Mam and Colleen were silent, but a constant string of songs from Christopher made fellow passengers smile kindly at him. Other children made faces at him and screwed a finger to their foreheads and stuck their tongues out in annoyance, but he ignored them and continued to entertain the adults, who were grateful for the distraction. Rain beat down on the windows, turning the lush landscape to a dull green.

It was dark when they got into Ballygarvan as the driver drove into the yard of Carberry's Hotel. At two long tables, everyone got fried eggs, slices of bacon and potato cakes with a smear of butter melting on top, and large teapots were passed up and down the table.

Christopher hummed on the next leg of the journey as well. Colleen thumped him a few times, but Mam grabbed her hand and said, 'Oh darling, leave him alone; he's happy enough and sure that's maybe the best way to be.'

'Mam, I'm so frightened,' whispered Colleen.

Mam tucked her daughter's head against her shoulder and stroked her face until she fell asleep. 'You're a good boy, Christopher,' she said to her son, and tickled him on the head. 'Is there no tune you don't know how to sing?' she added.

'He's a great entertainer altogether,' said an old man who talked to his fellow passengers in a low drone, inventing as much news as he dared and repeating over and over the little he actually knew about the shipwreck.

Mam closed her eyes, longing for the journey to end.

CHAPTER 29

THE DROWNED
AND THE SAVED

O n entering Kinsale the omnibus followed the Pier Road to the quays. The crowd rushed out of the vehicle and over to the quayside where a group of about a dozen survivors stood shivering in blankets near the doorway of a stone boathouse. Outside the boathouse were braziers with blazing turf and coal that gave off spurts of sparks as the wind changed direction. The survivors who shuffled about in ill-fitting but dry clothes were too shocked to answer the questions of those who had travelled from Queenstown and Cork. A nurse brought out a tray of tin mugs with soup and another woman a tray of buttered slices of bread. There was no shortage of food and it was all free. Mrs Kennedy and the children were very hungry and ate their fill.

Mam approached a survivor and managed to get his full attention. The Kennedys listened eagerly to the man who had one blanket tied around him like a kilt, another worn over his shoulders as a cloak. He shook his head: No, he knew nothing of Captain Kennedy or of Finbar. They left him and then saw a Cunard official writing up survivors' names in chalk on a blackboard. Mam's eyes quickly focused on the Ks: Frank Kellett, George Kessler, Herb Kienzle, Bill Kimball. No Kennedys.

'If you cannot find your loved ones here,' said the official to the crowd, 'you should go to the shed and search among the ...' he lowered his voice '... dead'. Mam put a hand to her mouth as he pointed across the quayside to a building with small fishing boats upturned outside it. She told Colleen to mind Christopher, then she walked slowly over to the door. Another official stood at the entrance with two constables who had several lanterns; they held out one to her and she took it, and went inside, her heart beating fast.

A long line of bodies lay on the ground like people in a deep, silent sleep. Two rows of them. The air had a faint smell of a fish market – of salt, sea spray and seawater. She raised the lantern high and looked around. She passed by the women's bodies quickly, knowing them by their features and matted hair. She paused before each man and before a boy dressed in a check suit. Not Finbar, but she held the lantern to his face twice, just to be sure. It took a long time for her to reach the last man: no, the man was short, clean-shaven, quite young. Not her husband at all.

'Is this the only place like this in Kinsale?' she asked one of the constables outside, handing back the lantern and staring into the crowd of onlookers across from the morgue.

'Only place? Well, yes,' he said. 'I think you should go to Queenstown, madam. I have been told to tell everyone if you do not discover what you need to know in Kinsale ...' he began to stumble over his words, 'you should go to Queenstown, ma'am.' He looked at her kindly.

'But I am from Queenstown,' said Mrs Kennedy in desperation as her children ran over to hug her.

'And did you search there for your loved ones?' said the constable.

'No. Not in any place like this,' she gestured with a hand at the makeshift morgue.

'The Cunard company can offer to accommodate you overnight in Kinsale,' he told her. 'And the omnibuses will be running again tomorrow. There is so much confusion, ma'am. We have never had to cope with such a situation, such a tragedy. We are confused too.' The constable stepped aside to let another woman in to begin her sad search.

CHAPTER 30

GOOD NIGHT

It was a very long journey back to Cork for Mam, with Christopher and Colleen sharing one seat beside her in the overcrowded omnibus. The children swung from being sad and weepy to being restless and teasing each other. The train for Queenstown was late and overcrowded. The whole world suddenly seemed to be going to Queenstown, Mam thought.

In Queenstown, there was a huge crowd milling about. Newspaper boys carried bulky bundles under their arms and chanted the news loudly: 'Sunk by German U-boat – read all about it.'

The Kennedys pushed their way out of the station where they saw printed billboard signs displayed inside latticing: *Cunard Information Office: Survivors, Advice, Information.* The temporary resting place of the drowned was a warehouse on the quayside. Thin blankets on the windows let in a dull light, with dusty beams on some of the faces, making them look like damp, pale, marble statues. Their arms lay folded across their stomachs or by the sides of their stiff, cold bodies. Again she looked at every face up close; each time apprehension left her as she did not recognise who it was.

'Let's go home,' she said, coming out into the sunshine at last into the noisy, chattering crowd – the newspaper vendors, soldiers, constables and seamen all surrounded by small groups of townsfolk unaffected by personal loss.

'Mam, did you see Daddy or Finbar?' Colleen looked up at her.

'No, darling, but it is all very sad,' Mam replied, and could not see her daughter for the tears.

'Do you think they're both drowned?' Colleen too started to weep.

'I hope not, Colleen love, but I couldn't find them and I cannot do anymore today.' Mam walked slowly up the hill, her children following her.

'But it's good that you didn't find them, isn't it, Mam?' Colleen took her mother's hand.

Christopher suddenly burst out: 'They'll be home, Mam,

186

I know it!' He grabbed her hand and sang all the way home.

Mrs Kelly listened to their news, then put on the kettle. 'What about a cup of tea, Kitty, and some apple tart?'

Mam was so distracted she began cutting the pie in so many slices she cut some of them twice over. Tears spilled from her eyes, and she said in a low voice to Mrs Kelly: 'The children love your baking.'

'Your mother is always fibbing,' Mrs Kelly tried to joke as she warmed the teapot. 'Your mother is a far better baker than I could ever be.' The twins smiled, but Colleen couldn't be distracted by smalltalk.

'I want to know where Daddy and Finbar are. I'm not very hungry, Mrs Kelly,' Colleen rushed upstairs.

'I love apple tart.' Christopher's voice was low. He took a huge slice and handed another to Sean. Mrs Kelly and Mam smiled at the young boys for a moment. It was their only smile that day.

In Kinsale, I went to a stone building marked 'Lusitania'. There were clusters of bottles, holding daffodils, on both sides of the entrance. I stared in. The bodies were in here, I soon discovered.

'What's your name, young fella?' a man asked, extending a hand to me, but I could hardly speak. 'You need dry clothes, lad,' the man said. He pointed to a shed. 'Over there.'

'I need to find my Dad,' I explained, and the man stood aside, and handed me a lantern. The warehouse was damp and dark, but I wasn't afraid after what I had experienced at sea. I moved from one drowned person to the next, checking for my father, and suddenly fell to my knees in front of Penny Mayberry. My chest heaved and I wept quietly, holding my stomach.

She was in her blazer and pinafore, her feet bare as the night she had talked in her cabin before she pushed them into her slippers. Only two nights ago, I thought, two nights! I put my knuckles into my mouth and bit hard, trying to stop the awful pain. Her face was like white marble – cold, bare, beautiful and gaunt. Her eyes were like jewels, staring at the ceiling and her blond hair was matted with sprigs of seaweed making a crown on her head. Her hands had been laid across her stomach with the fingers wedged together; they looked like polished ivory twigs.

I leant over her face and touched her on one cheek. It was like a piece of frozen ice, so cold I thought my fingers would stick to her.

'Oh Penny! Penny Mayberry!' The tears flowed down my face. I begged of the heavens that she would wake and call me 'Finny' and that we could talk and that she would tell me things were 'critical'. I stayed with her a very long time, unable to leave her behind forever. In the end, I spoke to her.

'Good night, sweet girl,' I said, as loud as I could. I said 'good night' even though it was morning, because in here night seemed more accurate because everything and everyone was dark and silent.

When I went outside eventually, I told the attendant that I could identify one of the drowned. The man took the details and asked me to specify which category the person was in: family, friend, crew, passenger?

'Passenger and ...' I nearly choked on my tears '... friend.' I could hardly say the word it meant so much to me.

The attendant stared. 'What was the relationship of the deceased to you, again?' The man held his pencil, poised to write. 'Here, boy, what is your name?'

'I am Finbar 'Finny' Kennedy and Penny Mayberry was my special friend,' I said and ran off in tears.

'Hey!' shouted the attendant, 'go and get dry clothes then go to the Cunard office', he pointed, 'and tell them who she is. You'll get help there too.'

I moved away from the crowd and walked to the side of the quay to where the water lapped the cut stone as I stared out to sea. I gathered my strength, went to the shed and found some dry clothes, then went to the Cunard office. A man behind the desk asked me to write a short report. They gave me a stool under a ledge and I limped over to it, where others were writing their reports too. I couldn't finish my sentences and sometimes began with '... then I, then I ...'. The clerk at the desk helped me phrase the whole statement and noted that I was Captain Kennedy's son. The positive identification of Penny Mayberry was of great help to the Cunard office, the clerk told me in a low voice. He handed me a voucher for food and a ticket for transport to Queenstown.

'One final thing, sonny,' the clerk said. 'Is this the correct address: 1 Park Terrace, Queenstown?'

'That's my home. Is my Dad, John Kennedy, a survivor?'

'You asked me that already, son, but all I can tell you is that he is not on the Kinsale list. You will be able to find out in Queenstown, where they have another list. There is still hope, son.' The clerk shook hands with me and said, 'Good luck, sonny.'

CHAPTER 31

THE SAD FAMILY

The Kennedy house was very quiet. The evening grew dark and the gaslights came on along Park Terrace, making the trees look like black shadows. Colleen woke in her bed; her chest hurt from weeping and she got up slowly and came downstairs. Mam rose in her chair in expectation, then slumped back down. Sean was asleep in the big chair with his head against one arm. Christopher was at the table, cutting out the photographs from the *Daily Sketch* about the *Lusitania* and when Colleen saw him, she gave her mother an angry look. Mam put a finger to her lips and shook her head, smiling at the boy.

'We're all up! We may as well have some tea,' said Mam. She made tea, then boiled some eggs that Mrs Kelly had left.

Suddenly a large shadow loomed in the panes of glass of the front door, and there was much shuffling outside. Someone in the street tugged the key on its length of cord through the letterbox and fumbled at the lock.

Mam ran at the door. 'Oh my God!' she screamed and almost fell backwards against the stairs. 'Oh my God!'

The children ran out to see who was there.

'Daddy. Daddy. Daddy. Daddy. Daddy!' shouted Christopher. 'I knew it! I knew you'd come back. Oh Daddy, you're home!'

'Daddy, I thought you ...' began Colleen, bursting into tears and running towards him, flinging her arms around his waist.

'My Daddy is back,' shouted Sean, waking up and nearly falling over as he ran to his father.

They all threw themselves at him and nearly knocked him to the ground in a wave of love.

'But where's Finbar?' Colleen stood back from her father.

'Listen, Colleen darling, I don't know where Finbar...' Captain Kennedy's eyes filled with tears and they all stared at him.

'Oh my God, Jack,' Mrs Kennedy said in shock, 'Finbar's not with you? And your poor arm! What happened?'

'The hand was mangled. That's where I've been – in a Cork hospital. The hand is useless now and I'll have to do without the use of it. But I'm lucky, I've only lost the use of my right arm. So many lost their lives. Let's sit down a moment. I cannot believe Finbar's not here. Oh my lovely son ...' He slowly began to tell them how he had survived, but his voice was low and mournful.

They crowded around him at the table and Mam sat beside him, holding his injured hand. They listened intently, looking at his face as he told them of all the horror of that dreadful day on the sea and how he had survived.

'... When the ship tipped over I was standing with Captain Turner and then we saw one of the rafts – it must have been the very last one – drop down on the deck in front of us. It was a miracle. As he was the Captain, we were the last to leave the ship – I think. I truly thought I was gone. My hand had been trapped under falling rubble when the ship collapsed, so Captain Turner had to drag me into the raft and he had to do all the rowing. It took hours, but we made it. It broke our hearts to see all the dead bodies in the sea – our precious passengers and crew. I stared and stared, looking for Finbar and when I didn't see him I just hoped and prayed ...'

CHAPTER 32

WHERE IS FINBAR?

Arriving back in Queenstown was a very strange experience for me, having left it as a runaway. That was all like a dream to me now and seemed so long ago. The Cunard offices were open and I read the list of survivors there. I burst into tears when I saw my father's name.

I limped along the quays and awkwardy climbed the steps past the cathedral as the bells chimed twelve midnight. I passed Fitz's grocery shop and hurried on as fast as my sore leg would carry me to No. 1 Park Terrace.

The house was dark, but I knocked and knocked and knocked until I thought the door would fall down. I forgot all about the key on the string, I was so upset. I had run away from home – and look at what happened. Would they want me back? Would my father really be there?

Mam opened the door. She dropped the candle she was holding and screamed. 'Oh, tell me it is you, Finbar, not some ghost!'

'It's Finbar, Mam.' I could not see her for tears. 'Mam, I'm sorry I ran away on ye, but I will explain–'

She rushed towards me and enveloped me in a hug. 'Oh Finbar, Finbar!' she cried.

By now the whole household was awake and downstairs. The others surrounded me and Mam, all of them weeping and hugging me and each other. Sean and Christopher were shouting at the tops of their voices: 'Finbar's home!' Colleen wrapped her arms around my neck and would not let go. Mam and Dad touched me all over as if I were broken and they were searching for the broken pieces. Mam lifted my hurt leg onto a chair to examine it. I started to explain all about the Seal Man, but Mam and Dad told me to shush – it didn't matter how I got there, all that mattered was that I was home.

Mam stoked up the fire, got the kettle on and brought out a pie. 'We'll have to celebrate Finbar's homecoming,' she said.

Dad put a stop to my apologies and excuses for running away. 'You're a man of the world, now, Finbar,' he said. He explained the loss of the use of his hand and said it was something he could live with. 'Finbar, you are my right hand now.' He laughed loudly. 'I won't be going to sea again. Captain Turner is going to recommend me for a desk job here in Queenstown in the Cunard office. Isn't that something? I'll be home for tea every night, for a change. And you can go back to school, Finbar.'

'And I do want to get back to school, Dad. Will Mr Dempsey kill me?' I asked, but I wasn't really afraid. 'And I'll keep working as a tout down at the quays and find other work so we won't be poor. And look!' I fidgeted in my pocket and pulled out a roll of dollars that had survived the sea. 'Mam, count them. It is a present from New York and from the *Lusitania* and from the Atlantic. It will all add up to a pretty penny.' I handed them to Mam and she wept again.

'Oh my gosh, there's twenty-eight dollars here! A fortune!' she said. She put her arms around me.

'We are not poor, Finbar,' said Dad. 'I am the richest man in the whole world. We have a roof over our heads and we are all together.' He looked around and smiled at us all – his precious family. 'We're not poor, and even if we are, we are happy and that's what matters. Our happiness will enable us to survive. There's Mam, Colleen, Finbar, Christopher, Sean and myself – the six of us in our own liner – with our troubles, indeed, but the best of weather whatever the weather. The finest ship I have ever sailed. And what is the name of this ship, crew?' Dad looked at all of us in turn.

'Tell us, Jack.' Mam was cutting more slices of pie.

'*The Survivor.*'

'REMEMBER THE LUSITANIA!'

HISTORICAL NOTE

REAL CHARACTERS IN THE BOOK

Aleister Crowley was a double agent. He worked for both the British and the Germans during the war. He was a writer and a member of many secret societies.

Captain Turner was the real captain of the *Lusitania* and gave evidence at the inquests into the sinking of the ship.

William Pierpont was the detective on board the *Lusitania*.

Paul König and *Gustav Stahl* were crew members and also German spies.

Walther Schwieger, the captain of the German U-20 which sank the *Lusitania*, was a war ace. He sank a further thirteen British ships. Schwieger and his crew died in 1917 when their U-boat exploded in a collision with a minefield.

Hooper, Schwieger's dog, was on board the U-20 when it hit the *Lusitania*.

All other characters are invented.

REAL PLACES AND THINGS

All contemporary locations and streets are real.

Weir's Boarding House in New York was real.

The newspaper offices and their publications were real.

The warning notice printed in the *New York Times* was real, and was believed to have been drafted by Aleister Crowley.

REMEMBER THE LUSITANIA!

'*Remember the Lusitania*' and '*Avenge the Lusitania*' were slogans used on recruiting posters to persuade young men, especially Americans, to enlist as soldiers in 1917 in the First World War (known as the Great War, 1914–1918).

The sinking of the *Lusitania* was a huge event in world news in May 1915. Only three years before, in 1912, the *Titanic* had sunk, with great loss of life, having struck an iceberg on its maiden voyage from Southampton, England, to New York. The *Titanic* disaster was explainable in terms of human error. The *Lusitania* disaster was not an accident.

On 7 May 1915 this great liner was sunk in an attack by a German submarine off the Irish coast near Kinsale. Close to 1,200 people died; two hundred of these were US citizens; six hundred were British and Canadian citizens.

There was huge public reaction to the sinking of the *Lusitania* and this meant that America eventually decided to join in the Great War.

DESIGN FLAWS

The bulkheads of the *Lusitania* were placed in such a way that the lower deck would be flooded if the ship was hit by a torpedo. This is what happened.

PLOTS AND CONSPIRACIES

The Germans torpedoed the *Lusitania*, and everyone knew that. However, another story slowly began to emerge. Down through the years people have tried to unravel that story, but it still remains a mystery to this day.

The claim is that the sinking was not just a lucky strike by a German submarine, but was really a plan drawn up by high-ranking officials in the British Navy and their spies in order to bring America into the war.

Walther Schwieger's diary states that the U–20 under his command sank the *Lusitania* on May 7 (1915). However, the day before, 6 May, Schwieger and the U-20 sank two other ships, *Candidate* and *Centurion*, and on 5 May sank the *Earl of Lathom*. All of these ships were hit in the sea south of Cobh and off the Wexford coast. The British Admiralty knew of these three sinkings yet they sent no warning to Captain Turner on the *Lusitania*. It is also on record that in March 1915 the Admiralty gave battleship protection to the *Lusitania* on entering and leaving Irish waters, but then withdrew it, so that in May there was no such support.

ARMS, AMMUNITION AND GOLD

Arms and other war supplies as well as gold bullion were part of the cargo of the *Lusitania*.

INQUESTS

There were two inquests after the disaster. They differ in several details.

Captain Turner, questioned in Kinsale in May 1915, spoke of only one torpedo which struck the liner at 2.15pm on the day of the disaster. The *Lusitania* sank eighteen minutes later.

Turner was evasive in answers about the British Admiralty's orders transmitted by Morse Code, which asked him to slow his speed long before the attack by the U-boat. The *Lusitania* was ordered to slow to 15 knots along the south Irish coast. The *Lusitania's* top speed was 25 knots, and travelling at 15 knots made it an easier target for the U-boat. Why was Captain Turner ordered to slow his speed? 'That is a matter for the Admiralty,' was the captain's rather weak answer, but it suggests that the *Lusitania's* passage through the war zone was controlled by the Admiralty, not the Captain of the liner.

At the second inquest in June 1915, Sir Edward Carson, acting for the British Navy, broke Turner down as the main witness. Carson put it to Turner that the *Lusitania* had been struck by two, even possibly three torpedoes. They wanted to prove that the sinking was completely due to torpedoes and not to any arms already on board the ship. Turner agreed that two torpedoes had struck the *Lusitania*, contradicting what he had said at the earlier inquest. But in later years he stated publicly that only one torpedo had struck the ship; this is also what Schwieger, the captain of the German U-20, said in his accounts of the shipwreck.

The London inquest stated that the reason for the reduction in speed was to enable the *Lusitania* to arrive in Liverpool in a good tide. But this seems unconvincing: it could have slowed down nearer to Liverpool and would have had battleship protection within English shores.

These mysteries remain unanswered to this day.

OTHER BOOKS
from

Spirit of the Titanic
Nicola Pierce

The ghost of fifteen-year-old Samuel Scott moves
restlessly aboard the *Titanic* as she sails to her doom
in 1912. An eyewitness to the final days in the lives
of rich and poor, crew and passengers,
this is Samuel's story.
'This breathtaking book takes you on the deck of
the *Titanic* with its amazing descriptive language
describing every scene from top to bottom...'
Guardian Children's Books Online

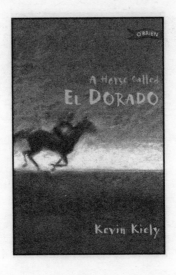

A Horse Called El Dorado
Kevin Kiely

Pepe loves to gallop across the plains of Colombia
on his horse, El Dorado. Then the guerrillas come,
and Pepe has to move to Ireland to live with his
grandparents. How will he cope? Will he ever find a
horse as wonderful as his beloved El Dorado?